HAPPINESS
in a HOAX
A MILITARY ROMANCE

CLAIRE CAIN

Cover design by Jess Mastorakos - Jess@jessmastorakos.com

E-Book ISBN: 978-1-954005-34-1

Print book ISBN: 978-1-954005-35-8

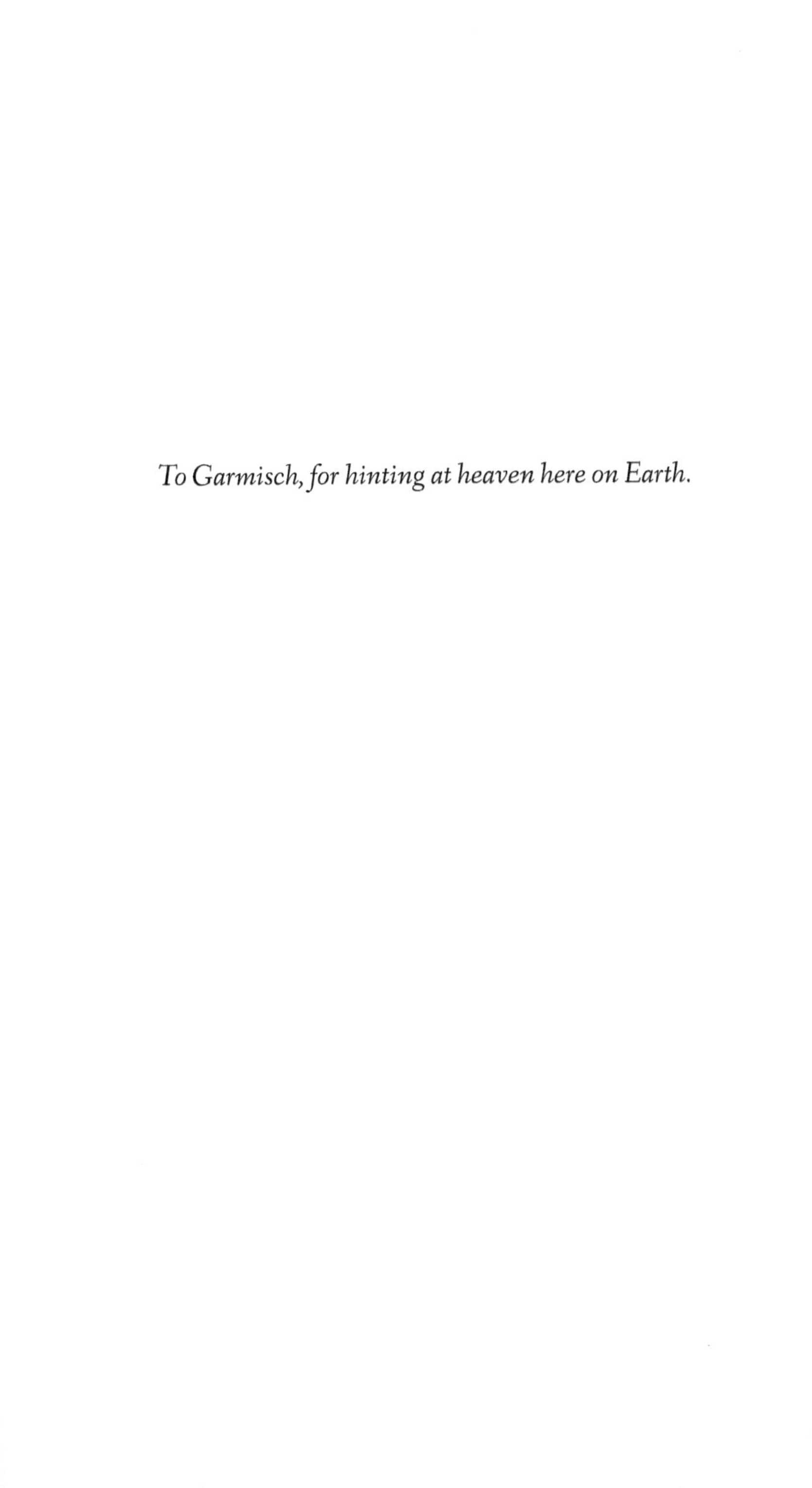

To Garmisch, for hinting at heaven here on Earth.

CONTENT WARNING

Dear reader,

Happiness in a Hoax is a sweet military romance about two people falling in love while engaged in a marriage of convenience. While it's generally lighthearted, it may contain content not suitable for some readers.

The heroine's background includes an abusive upbringing. This book takes place many years after that situation has come to an end, but she does work through some of her feelings and memories as she interacts with the hero. The hero is briefly held captive (prologue only) and is then released with some physical and emotional injuries.

I hope readers who find this content to be particularly sensitive can make the best decision for their health and happiness. I want you to walk away with only happy, lovely feelings, and I hope you'll feel safe proceeding with this information in mind. If you have questions or need more information, contact me at claire@clairecainwriter.com.

My very best to you,
Claire

NOTE FROM THE AUTHOR

This series focuses on soldiers stationed overseas. OCONUS is the military acronym that stands for Outside the Continental United States. So really, it's what military personnel say when they're stationed somewhere other than the 48 continental states.

Any posting in Germany is an OCONUS duty station.

This series was formerly titled the OCONUS Bonus Series, but since that's not very clear for civilian readership, we've got a fresh series title. I couldn't skip this little intro, though, because the OCONUS setting is such a big part of the series. Being a service member outside the US is unique!

I hope you'll enjoy a peek at my fictionalized version of being stationed in Germany, which is based on my time living in Bavaria as a military spouse—truly some of my favorite years so far.

PROLOGUE

"*Charlie team, go.*"

The team moved silently through the darkness to breach the doors. In seconds, they'd subdued one guard, eliminated every other enemy occupant of the holding cell, and located the prisoners.

"Execute," Charlie Zero-Six said low into his mic.

His team of ten moved quickly, all efficiency and focus. The men they'd come for were unconscious, so they moved to ID them by known identifying marks. Zero-Two found the scar on the back of the captain's hand, and Zero-Three found the tattoo on the sergeant's bicep. After a brief check by the medic, they secured the two prisoners on fold-out sleds, and two-man teams moved the unconscious bodies back the way they came in.

"Ex-fil, Ex-fil, Ex-fil." Zero-Six's call to the birds came while they navigated back to the exit.

They left the small Taliban compound and moved to the Blackhawk helicopters landing as they arrived. They loaded one soldier and half the team, along with the team leader, onto one bird.

"Zero-One, take Miller." Zero-Six flicked a gloved hand toward the other helicopter, where two members of the four-man group loaded Sergeant Miller.

"Roger." West—aka Zero-One—followed the sled on, with East behind him. The pilot lifted the bird before their boots had fully left the ground.

"He's out good. I'm starting a line. West, talk pretty for me." South spoke into his helmet mic, swiping the inside of the lifeless arm with antiseptic before starting an IV.

West leaned in, pulling his eye protection and mic away from his face so he wouldn't scare the man when he woke. He'd done that one too many times, and it saved the target a lot of terror if they weren't confronted by a masked and unidentifiable figure upon waking from unconsciousness.

"All right, buddy, wake up for me. Let me see your eyes." He spoke at a yell, shaking the man's chin just slightly, though not enough to disturb South's work.

No answer came, unsurprisingly, so he kept at it over South's string of expletives about nonexistent veins due to extreme dehydration.

"Time to get up, Sergeant Miller. Good guys got you, and you've got a wife to get home to, don't you?"

North nodded, though they all knew the details on both men. They memorized dossiers full of information on each soldier so they'd be prepared for anything.

"Your wife's gonna want to see you, Miller. And I hear you live in Germany—cush assignment, man. Let me see those baby blues for a minute, and we'll get you home."

The man gasped, and his eyes shot open, unfocused and wild. His arms jerked up before West and South subdued him.

"You're all right. You made it out. You're gonna be fine."

West patted the flag at his chest and Miller's eyes focused there, flicked to West's, then rolled back and shut again.

CHAPTER ONE

Katie

The flight attendant dimmed the lights and I shut my eyes, knowing I needed sleep. I had no idea what would happen upon my arrival in Germany, or what any of this meant.

The moment everything changed came tunneling back in my memory.

"Ma'am, your husband has been extracted. We're flying you to Germany to meet him at the hospital."

They'd knocked on my door eight days ago with the news that Noah had been abducted during what they believed to be a planned attack against American soldiers in a southern province of Afghanistan. The Taliban took the two men—one of them Noah—after separating them from the larger group. As of about twelve hours ago, Noah's boss, the man I spoke to most often, notified me a team had successfully rescued him.

After waking hours before to the news I'd been praying for, I could hardly remember the rest of the day. Now, I sat crunched between passengers on a flight halfway across the Atlantic, en route to see my husband after not having seen the man in almost two years.

I didn't know how to act or even what to *think*. They wouldn't tell me specifics about injuries or any details, only that they'd speak to me when I got there, and that I could see him when I landed at Ramstein Air Base in Germany.

My mind wandered right to Noah while my heart ached. It might've been all in my head, or it might have really been hurting, but I missed him. It was stupid, of course, but I'd missed him. And now, knowing he'd been in peril for more than a week—whether he was alive or dead, uncertain—I missed him in the bone-deep way I rarely let myself feel.

I never let myself experience the love and admiration I would so easily fall into if I didn't watch it. What a stupid thing that would be, right? Loving my husband.

Except the one thing no one knew—no one but Noah's mom, me, and Noah himself—was an undeniable truth. And that truth held the reason it made no sense for me to love him, to want him, to miss him, or to wish to be with him. It had motivated me to banish all those feelings five years ago—and whenever they popped up along the way—and do whatever I could to keep them gone.

Noah had married me to save me from harm. He'd married me because he was too kind and good, and when his mother had given him the idea, he'd done it without a second thought. And now, almost five years in, we still didn't know each other—not really. We'd spent a handful of days together, max. Mostly, we'd lived our lives separately, which had always been the plan.

And yet, I'd been listed as his primary contact on his military documents, not his mother. I'd asked if they'd contacted his mom, and his commander, Lieutenant Colonel Wolfe, had said he'd authorized it only because of the unique nature of the situation, but that the Army would only fly me to be with him.

I swallowed down the rising panic and exhaled, willing the pressure in my chest to ease. But it kept coming back, right along with the inability to breathe normally or think straight anytime I thought of how terrified he must have been or wondered what it was like. Had they beaten him? Starved him? Shot him?

Please, God, no.

And then the other thoughts came. Would he recognize me when I showed up? We hadn't seen each other in a long time, only e-mailed or texted. It wasn't like we traded photos or stalked each other online.

The last time we'd met in person had only been for a few hours, just to go to the legal department to sign updated wills and get me a power of attorney before he deployed again. I didn't need many since his assets would go to his mother, but I had to have access to our shared accounts and a few other things that got tricky if I needed something while he was gone.

He'd gotten home from that same deployment while final exams monopolized my brain and time, so I hadn't seen him. I'd felt guilty about that. I'd wanted to see him, but he'd refused to push in on my study schedule. He'd promised me it was no big deal and told me not to worry, to study hard, and to ace my tests. Then he'd assured me he couldn't wait to get to Germany, his next duty station.

The last time he'd seen me, I'd been twenty-one. It'd been two years since, and I didn't keep a social media pres ence like he did—nothing my family could use to find me, even still. They would be looking for Katie Simonsen, not Katie Miller, but I didn't need to make it easier for them either. Also, now my hair was shorter and darker. I'd looked almost fully blond the last time he'd seen me. I'd lost weight in places and gained it in others. Would he like that?

Doesn't matter, stupid.

The jerk in my head had been spewing hateful things ever since they notified me days ago. I'd worked hard over the years to get past the drowning sensation that came whenever anything went wrong.

I'd talked to my therapist, Maria, once a day since they'd called, bless her. And still, here it was, rearing its head.

I knew, logically, I bore no blame for Noah's capture. Nothing I did—no amount of worrying or crying or begging God—could change that it'd happened. I believed prayer might help him be recovered in Afghanistan, but those other things? No. They wouldn't. The voice berating me, telling me it was all my doing and that if I'd just been a better wife none of this would have happened? Nonsense.

I knew it, and yet, I couldn't block it out.

It's all your fault. It's all your fault. It's all your fault.

Sometimes, it sounded like my stepfather's voice. Other times, my stepbrother's. And the worst was when it was my own voice, which proved to be the hardest to ignore. I tried to think about what my therapist had reminded me earlier today. I breathed it in while blocking out the person next to me. He shifted in his seat and jostled the whole row while children and babies cried from different corners of the packed *Stars and Stripes Express* flight for military personnel and their families.

Maria had asked, "Would you talk to a friend this way?"

"Of course not!"

She only had to give me that look of hers that told me I should draw my own conclusion, and I knew. I wouldn't speak to a friend this way. I wouldn't tell a friend that the Taliban had captured her husband—something I didn't even know happened anymore—because of her. Never.

So why are you talking to yourself this way?

I exhaled again, letting my lungs empty completely, and then pulled in a breath slowly and steadily until air—not stress or fear—filled my chest.

The real Mrs. Miller, Noah's mom, had called me twice. I'd been too much of a basket case to answer the first time and at work with my phone tucked away the second. I'd texted her back, sharing her hope that we'd hear good news soon. It struck me that I hadn't told her about the flight plans, or anything about my trip here   it'd all been so whirl-wind. I'd had hours to prepare. I'd messaged her to say they'd rescued him, but after that...

I'd always assumed he'd list his mom as his primary contact, not me. In fact, I was pretty sure during that first deployment or so, he'd listed his mom as such. It didn't make sense for it to be me—I had nothing to offer him and owed him everything.

I forced away those thoughts, the fear and genuine worry that I had no idea how to act in this situation, and started the count. From one thousand back to one, and I'd repeat it if I had to until I got some sleep. I wouldn't think about him not recognizing me, or how bad this could be if anyone noticed how nervous and unprepared I was. I wouldn't think how quickly everything could crash and burn.

∼

"This way, ma'am." Sergeant Wilkins gestured to the van idling at the curbside, door open.

I followed his direction, bleary from the nine-hour flight. I was surprised to notice he stood a few inches shorter than me and had an extremely warm face and a kind smile. My suitcase rattled behind me when I stepped to the curb. "Uh, I'll just take my—"

"I'll get that for you, ma'am." Chaplain Tate, the man about my height who looked not much older than me, had met me along with Sergeant Wilkins at the welcome area of the small Air Force airport. He took my giant, busted-looking suitcase from my hand before I could ask what to do with it.

"Oh, thanks."

Obviously, it should go in the back. What kind of person tries to put that size of a bag on their lap?

Exhaustion engulfed me. I was so, so tired. And yet everything around me stood out in sharp relief. The sense of surrealism shimmered at the edge of my vision like it'd evaporate soon and I'd be back in my studio apartment just eight —or was it technically nine now?—days ago, arriving home from work, and in that alternate version of the story, I wouldn't get the knock on the door that ruined my ability to function.

I slid into the first row of the van. Sergeant Wilkins sat behind me and Chaplain Tate jumped into the passenger seat. I hadn't met the driver, but I wasn't sure I had room for much more information if it didn't directly have to do with Noah.

The van doors slammed, and I clutched my purse to my chest, wishing it'd bring some sense of comfort or normalcy, but knowing the racing heart and slippery feeling in my brain wouldn't subside until I saw him.

Until I could touch him and see him and know he was safe. *That* part, the role of a concerned person who loved this man, I could do. It might not look quite like a wife reuniting with her husband, but I didn't need to fake concern or care.

"So right now, we're going to get you settled in a room here at the Ramstein Inn. We'll give you an hour or so to freshen up, and then we'll shuttle you to the hospital. It's just a few minutes away. Visiting hours haven't started yet, so there's no rush."

My chest tightened at the thought of waiting another hour. "I can't see him until visiting hours, I guess?"

Sergeant Wilkins's smile was soft and full of regret. "Unfortunately, no."

They must have chosen him because he exuded kindness and calm, both he and the chaplain. Though you'd kind of expect that from a chaplain. Or I supposed you might. I didn't know. I'd never met an Army chaplain before.

"Okay. Well, that's great then. I'll get cleaned up and wait for you?"

He nodded, but the chaplain spoke from the front seat. "We'll be right on time, ma'am. I had a chance to visit with Noah yesterday, and I know they're hoping that seeing you will help him."

Little crumbles of rocky anxiety dropped into my stomach as I swallowed and nodded, hoping the fear that must be shining in my eyes didn't betray me. Of course, it was normal for me to be scared, but I didn't know if seeing me would help. I hated that these men would likely see the moment it did or didn't make a difference.

I sucked in a breath, and it must have been audible because the chaplain gave me one of those frown-smiles that would sound something like *aw, honey,* and Sergeant Wilkins patted my shoulder.

"He's going to be all right, ma'am. We'll get you to him just as soon as we can."

~

Hands shaking, I opened the door to his room, hardly able to breathe. They must've pulled all the oxygen from the air in here and piped it directly into the patients.

Because that makes so much sense.

A nurse in dark blue scrubs stood next to the bed, blocking my view of its occupant.

"All righty. I'll be back in a bit to check on you. Oh, looks like you have a visitor, so I'll get out of your hair."

The nurse turned and smiled brightly at me. I tracked her movement past me, then my eyes jumped to the man in the bed.

Tears hit my eyes while a deep ache punched into my ribs.

"Hi, Noah." My voice emerged small, even in the cramped hospital room.

"Hey, gorgeous." His low, deep voice sounded graveled and rough. It was thrilling and comforting, like always, with the slight Southern-accented pull to his words.

He opened a hand to me, palm up, where it rested on top of the blanketed bed. I moved closer and set my hand in his much larger, warm one.

"I'm so glad you're okay."

"Me too."

Light blue eyes that looked older than the last time I'd seen them watched me. Exhaustion clearly nagged at him. His jaw seemed more defined, and someone must have shaved his face at some point recently because he only had a dusting of stubble a bit darker and slightly red under his chin. His dark blond hair was a little longer than I'd seen it before, and even in the hospital bed, disheveled and uncombed, it looked great on him. Despite the past week inside, his skin looked tan as usual, and his cheeks appeared slim—not quite gaunt, but not normal either.

Finally registering his slumped posture and slow blinks, I said, "I can leave. I'll come back in a—"

"No, please. Sit." His fingers tightened around mine. "I'm glad you're here. They have me doped up on some pain meds so I'm sleepin' a ton, but I want you here."

"You do?" The whisper slipped out before I could stop myself. It surprised me to hear him say it outright. Or to hear him say it at all, really.

"I do. Thank you for comin'." His perfect lips pulled up into a closed smile. "Truly."

"I—I'm glad I'm here. Can I ask what happened? Or, I mean, not how it *all* happened, but why they have you on pain medication? Are you... okay?" I internally rolled my eyes at my stuttering and the world's stupidest question. *Hi, dear. You were taken captive by the Taliban and held for a week. Doing okay?*

"I'm fine. Had a mild concussion, severe dehydration, and bruised ribs, I think they said. Which is what they gave me the meds for. Also, somethin' with my right quad—severe bruising, I think? Won't be runnin' this next week or anything. IVs for nutrients and infection, which is probably overkill. Or maybe it's because I was dehydrated. But now I'm just... loopy."

"I'm so sorry, Noah. That's terrible." I pulled a chair close to the bed and sat, the specifics of his injuries providing both relief and a cruel amount of vivid detail that told me how poorly he'd been treated, especially considering they'd only held him for a little over seven days.

He didn't respond right away, but his gaze surveyed me. My brown hair was to my shoulders and a little wild because I hadn't done much other than dry it at the hotel after my shower. My face had filled out from when he'd last seen me.

"Could've been worse." His blink after that came slowly, and his eyes opened after a moment or two.

"You need sleep."

He nodded. "Glad you're here, honey."

CHAPTER TWO

Noah

The woman sitting by my bed had aged, and the years since I'd seen her had been nothing but kind.

Pardon my French, but damn, she was gorgeous. Not to sound trite, but she had blossomed.

I hadn't seen her in close to two years. She refused social media, which I couldn't fault her for, given her absolutely deranged family. But this meant I had no way of keeping tabs on her except for whatever she gave me, which came in little fits and starts via text or e-mail. Things like, *Just checking in to see how you're doing. Graduating with my bachelor's degree today!* Or, *Starting my first teaching job and I feel so nervous I could die! But then I remember all the crazy stuff you've done, and I figure teaching a bunch of kindergarteners shouldn't be that terrifying.*

You know—sweet, charming stuff. Just enough to keep me dangling on her hook, unable to consider a life outside of this odd married one. Not that I'd ever start a relationship with someone else while I had her ring on my finger, even if we'd both signed on for a marriage in name only. She might've had boyfriends, but I'd had no one. Nothing. Only her, thousands of miles away, living a life entirely separate from mine.

We'd agreed to that. We'd gotten married just after I'd turned twenty-one, and she was barely eighteen—literally. We married on her birthday. It was the day she could finally legally escape her family. Her bags were packed for days, I'd driven all night to get there, and we'd married at the court-house in downtown Centerville, Kentucky, the first appointment of the day.

Her birthday, and our fifth anniversary, was fast approaching. Hard to believe. Almost twenty-three looked good on her. And having her here with me, caring about me, that concern in her eyes and the downturn of her ridicu-lously thick, soft-looking lips...

"Are you feeling okay, Noah?"

The voice. The voice was good too—textured and almost rough, but still sweet-sounding. I'd noticed it the first time we spoke when she was sixteen. Right before her step-father had stormed up to the fence on his midnight horse where she sat talking with me, grabbed her by the arm, and jerked her away without even acknowledging my existence. Granted, I'd had no idea she was sixteen then, so I'd crushed hard on her, working to catch glimpses of her whenever I could. That'd been rare in the weeks after our first meeting, and after that, she'd kept her distance, much to my heart's and teenage hormone-addled brain's dismay.

"Huh? Yeah, just fine. Sorry. Spacin' out, I guess."

"Do you want me to grab a nurse?" She set her warm hand on my wrist.

"No, honey, it's all right. It's not the concussion. I was just thinkin' of that first time we met after y'all moved next door." Happily, it wasn't the concussion or the damn flashes of memory from the last week of my life I'd much rather forget.

"Oh... yeah. I remember that too." Her pale cheeks brightened to a fiery red, and she blinked away from me.

"Thinkin' about that embarrasses you?"

She withdrew her hand and glanced around the room before her eyes settled back with mine. "Partly. Lots of emotions mixed up in that memory for me."

I studied her, noticing her fingers twisting together and the way she bit her lower lip. A nervous habit? Sometimes, the strangeness of not knowing things like that about her struck me. Especially in a circumstance like now, when the chaplain would be coming to talk to me and my wife.

She was my *wife*.

Not exactly news, but having her here and functioning in that way was... different. Remarkable, but also a little terrifying. Surely, someone would realize the truth between us. And in a way, it was more than a little thrilling to have her belong to me here, in this room, in this moment.

I'd thought of her. Fleetingly, because I'd never viewed her as a viable option considering our agreement, and in the beginning, her age. Once I'd graduated high school and joined the Army, I'd worked to forget about her. But then Mom called, and I jumped in without thought.

She had always been the most beautiful girl I'd ever seen, and truth be told, she'd only become more and more lovely as time passed. I'd been so preoccupied with thoughts of her during my year-long deployment that I'd avoided seeing her before I moved to Germany. I was too afraid to see her and do something stupid like kiss her and tell her I wanted her, for real, and always had.

Moving to Germany had been a new leaf, so to speak. I'd worked to forget her. To live my life and pray she was finding joy and success between the messages that confirmed she was. Yet a year later, and two years after I'd last seen her, I'd thought of her each day during captivity in Afghanistan. I'd wondered if I'd get messages from her again, or if I'd die in that place. I'd had to remember what she looked like from our last meeting and wondered if she'd be okay without me, even though we'd been planning on divorcing soon, anyway.

Having her here hit me square in the gut in the best possible way. It filled my mind with *her* and our shared, odd past, freeing me just a bit from the cloud that'd hung over me as I came out of this nightmare.

"What kind of memories?" My voice was rough—both unused and textured with all the new awareness disorienting me.

Her forehead wrinkled in a frown while she inspected her hands. "Mostly the embarrassment of having my stepfather drag me away from you."

"Understandable. But that's not somethin' you need to be embarrassed about."

Her eyes snapped to mine.

"I know that." The sharp response seemed to startle her because she reached for my hand and squeezed it. "I'm sorry. I've worked through a lot of those feelings with my therapist, but they still crop up, and it's hard not to feel frustrated that I can't just... leave it all behind me. I guess I'm snippy from jet lag or something."

I set my free hand on top of hers, wincing as my arm

grazed my bruised ribs. "You're amazing. You don't need to explain anything to me."

Those big golden-brown eyes blinked back at me. "Okay."

This was the kind of moment that, if she were truly my wife, I'd tug on her hand a little and get her to move closer so I could kiss her. My heart rate ticked up and the monitor beeped.

"We doing okay in here?" Dr. Web burst through the door—or, hell, maybe she didn't burst in—but it felt like she burst *something* with her entrance.

"Yep. Just fine, Doctor."

"Is he telling the truth?" Dr. Web asked Katie, a conspiratorial brow raised in question.

"As far as I can tell," Katie answered, standing and moving out of the way before I could do anything about it.

Now that she was here, I wanted her with me. I didn't want her going back to the hotel at night, even though that thought was ridiculous. We'd never even spent the night together.

"Let me check you over and then I'll leave you two alone. I'm going to have you sit all the way up and—"

"I'll just step out for a few. I need some coffee." Katie gathered her purse and jacket, then reached for the door.

"It's fine for you to stay, ma'am." Dr. Web tucked the stethoscope into her ears and pressed the button to raise the bed, which immediately began shifting the surface under me.

"No, no, that's okay. Need anything, Noah, er, honey?" Her cheeks flushed as she backed out the door.

"Nah, baby, I'm fine. See you in a bit." I winked before she shut the door, then turned my attention to the doc, who proceeded to check me over—every bit of me—and I was glad Katie'd stepped out of the room when she did.

Not that I'd mind Katie seeing everything at some point, or that it would ever happen. But doing so when I'd dropped probably fifteen pounds and was weak, bruised, and generally unprepared? Not so much.

"You're good. I think we'll keep you one or two more days just to be sure we're not going to see any issues with the concussion. This afternoon, they're going to come talk with you about what happened now that you're not on the pain meds. So rest up, Sergeant."

"No other details you can recall?" John Corelli asked. He was supposedly a psychologist, though he seemed pretty beefy and fit for a guy who sat at a desk all day.

It'd been an hour of painstakingly recounting the events leading up to our capture. Not for the first time, wave after wave of humiliation and shame choked my words. I probably cleared my throat fifty times in that hour, forcing the descriptions out. It wasn't like I hadn't relived those moments a hundred times—maybe a thousand. While we were waiting to be rescued, hungry and trying not to lose hope, I'd gone over and over and *over* how they'd gotten us.

Despite everyone's reassurance it hadn't been my or Captain Waverly's fault, we'd both been grappling with the thought that we were to blame, at least in some small way.

"No, sir. I'm sorry. I wish I knew more, but they bagged us before we saw anything, then shoved us into the room where they held us for about an hour and a half."

I wished I could recall anything else that would help, but in the end, my best guess was that the operators who came and got us out had already taken care of the guys who'd caused the trouble.

"The guys who rescued us—did they get everyone in that compound?" I hated that I hadn't been conscious for the event. Some part of me needed to see the bodies of the men who'd beaten us. Who'd threatened our lives, our fellow soldiers' lives, and even our families.

Corelli squinted through his glasses and studied me. I met his stare, waiting to get any info out of him. So far, he'd only asked me questions and repeated the information Chaplain Tate had shared after I landed at Ramstein Air Base. I'd roused for a few minutes in the helicopter when the operator spoke to me, and I'd come to again when they were loading us onto a C-17 to make the flight from Kandahar to Ramstein. At that point, no one had told me much at all. They'd kept us separated from the other soldiers flying back, and I'd never even caught the guys' names that were supervising us. They were probably medics because I was pretty sure they sedated us, but maybe I'd just been out of it.

At Ramstein, Chaplain Tate and Sergeant Wilkins had escorted me and Rob—Captain Waverly—to the hospital. There, they'd given us the basics: they'd sent a strike team from a special operations unit to get us. They notified our families, and my wife and Waverly's parents were a few hours behind us, but en route. Waverly had a broken clavicle, broken ribs, and two broken fingers, so he'd been much more heavily sedated. He'd been whisked off to surgery after X-rays showed they couldn't fix his fingers without it.

I'd had a mild concussion, bruised ribs—though they thought one might be cracked—a bruised quad, and was pretty disoriented. Both of us had been malnourished. While in captivity, they'd given us a handful of something that seemed like protein bars over the seven days. But damn, had it felt like weeks. The shock of finding out it had only been seven was both a relief and a headbutt to my sternum.

I didn't remember much from the rescue except for when I came to and the operator was talking to me. *"You're all right. You made it out. You're gonna be fine."* Best words I'd ever heard.

"They did. But that brings me to the next thing. You'll need to sign this non-disclosure agreement."

I nodded and signed the document he slid toward me. I never would've anticipated needing to do that, especially since I remembered little of the team who'd recovered me and Waverly, but it made sense. They had to control the variables, their reputation, the information that got out about the Exceptional Mission Force.

Maybe this would give me some closure. Or at least a sense of completion to the series of events that made me feel ill and weak and useless just thinking about them.

At least Katie was here, though. I could focus on her and figure out how to avoid getting prosecuted for marriage fraud on top of everything else.

CHAPTER THREE

Katie

I'd barely slept since I'd arrived a little over two days ago, and now they planned to release him and drive us to the base where he was stationed.

To his house.

It wasn't ideal for me to stay in his room because he lived in the barracks since his housing allowance went to my rent back in North Carolina. But they'd coordinated with the small hotel on base and secured me a room there.

We'd only had a few moments alone, and they'd been... fine. He'd assured me, from that first moment, he was glad I had come. And so far, that seemed true.

He'd also explained why he'd listed me as his primary contact—one more effort to fly under the radar. Soldiers didn't have to list spouses as beneficiaries or primary contacts, which struck me as kind of messed up, but it gave people freedom. In the past, he'd always listed his mom as his point of contact, but he changed it last year when they started cracking down on fraud. His Command Sergeant Major made it his personal mission to root out couples doing anything seeming fraudulent, so Noah had been on high alert.

He talked to his mom on the phone daily and texted with her often, keeping her in the loop. It was something I'd admired about him—he respected her just as much as he loved her. I knew it even before I really knew him because I saw the way they interacted. It was so different from how my stepbrother or stepfather treated anyone. I'd never imagined a man was capable of that kind of tenderness without seeming weak, but Noah was the strongest person I could imagine.

"Did you get checked out of the hotel okay?" Noah asked when I peeked into his room.

"Yep. Ready to go. Everything ready here?"

I tucked my shaking hands into my pockets and stepped fully inside. I still hadn't gotten used to being near him. The shock of seeing him hooked to an IV in a hospital bed—in the wake of what he'd experienced—had diminished by the day. But generally, being around him still set me and my frayed ends on edge.

He stood from the side of the bed and stepped toward me. In that second, I realized I hadn't seen him out of bed—not once in the two-and-a-half days I'd been here. He'd always been sitting or lying down.

I'd forgotten how tall he was, how broad. How... *big*. And how much I liked that about him.

He stopped just in front of me, carefully watching my face like it held all the answers to an important problem he needed to solve. My breath caught and I didn't move. His nearness felt like a touch, even though a few inches separated us. It was like the air between us thickened and bridged the gap without our consent.

But he wasn't touching me. He was speaking, and I shook off the odd sensation and listened.

"Before we get in the van and we're surrounded by people for the next while, can I say somethin'?"

"Of course."

He placed a warm, large hand on my arm just above my elbow and ducked his head so our eyes met. "What I need to say might sound odd. So first, Katie, I need you to know how grateful I am you came all the way here. I never would've dreamed you'd do that, and I thank you."

The earnest tone, and maybe more so the sentiment of disbelief, made me speak without thinking. "Of course I'd come, Noah. How could I not?"

His brows dipped and he frowned a little.

"Well, I guess that's a good point. And soon enough, you'll be off the hook. But for now..." He cleared his throat but spoke even quieter. "I need everyone to believe this—believe we're in this. Sergeant Major Allen's been even more suspicious lately. So I just..."

A jolt of white-hot fear shot through me. "Of course. We'll be fine. You'll be fine."

He'd married me to help me out of a terrible situation, but it wasn't without a payoff for him—quite literally. The only way he and his mom had talked me into it had hung on him getting something from the arrangement too. The deal was, we'd live separately. I'd choose nice, but small, places to live, and he'd pocket the difference. The Army gave him BAH—Basic Allowance for Housing, which changed depending on where you lived. They calculated for where the spouse lived if the couple lived separately. I'd been living in Raleigh, but in a microscopic, rent-controlled studio apartment. So as he'd gone up in rank, there'd been more and more for him.

Technically, we were married. And he'd explained a long time ago that plenty of people did this—got married and used the setup to make money. Plus, the spouse got healthcare benefits, and it all worked out in the end.

Unless someone decided the marriage existed to defraud the Army. And while it was a fairly tricky thing to prove, there'd been a big exposé on the practice last year near Fort Bragg, which put us at risk. It contributed to why we'd planned to divorce after five years instead of sooner. He also wanted to make sure I had rent and healthcare covered, and no hindrances to getting through college, especially since being married to him got me a military discount on tuition.

I'd do whatever he needed me to in order to protect him. They'd made examples out of the couples in the article, and that always included an other-than-honorable discharge from the Army. Not something anyone wanted on their employment record.

His commander had called the hospital room and spoken to him every day. During one of those calls, he mentioned he'd give Noah leave so we could spend time together while he recuperated. Noah had hung up looking pale, but I'd heard the conversation.

"I can stay, no problem," I'd said without thinking, then immediately notified the school. We had arranged for my flight back, and the rest... Well, it wasn't history, but we'd see how it went.

I didn't know what would happen on this leave, but I'd planned to be gone around three weeks at least, especially since they hadn't given me much information about the extent of Noah's injuries before I flew out. The school had been generous, and fortunately, my long-term sub had been available for the rest of the year, just in case. I'd return less than two weeks before the end of the year. And while it made me sad to miss out on these last few weeks with the kids—potentially the last kids I'd ever have in my own classroom since I'd be moving to focus on my grad program in the fall—I felt like I owed Noah this.

Being with him on leave presented an entirely unheard-of scenario for our relationship. I had no idea what it meant, and I didn't know how I'd handle myself around him when every time we made eye contact, I felt tingly and stupid. So, I'd focus on the logistics and pray I wouldn't embarrass myself or him.

"Thank you. I'm sorry you're in this position." He slid his hand up my arm, over my shoulder, and gripped the back of my neck, a wave of goosebumps left in its wake.

I spoke around the thrill and the tendrils of nervous anxiety taking root in my belly. "You don't need to thank me, Noah. This is the very least I can do."

"Ready to go here?" Chaplain Tate knocked loudly on the wall near the door and smiled warmly. Standing in the same space next to Noah, he seemed almost petite. At five-foot-nine, I often had inches on my fellow woman, and I suspected Noah had the same experience with men since he stood an inch or two above six feet.

"We sure are." Noah's voice sounded downright cheery, and I wondered if it was real.

"Great. If you'll come with me, we'll jump in the van and get going. I don't want to run into a *stau* and have to check you in after hours."

The chaplain spoke like this should all make perfect sense, but of course, I had no idea what that word meant other than it rhymed with *wow* and had something to do with how long it would take to make it to the base where Noah lived.

"Oh, sure. But… what's a *stau*?"

Noah walked slowly next to me, following the chaplain down a long hallway to the elevators that would lead to the loading area. Sergeant Wilkins had already taken our bags.

"It's traffic, but a *stau* can literally last hours. Things will come to a total standstill, drivers will get out of their cars and pop open drinks. It's insane," Noah explained.

His hand brushed my lower back as we walked, and my stomach clenched at the contact. We'd touched so little over the years that every contact felt heightened.

The chaplain pressed the *down* button, waiting for the doors to close, and smiled again. "It's true. The longest one I've been in was six hours."

"*Six hours?!*"

Both he and Noah chuckled.

"Okay, well, let me hit the bathrooms before we go, just in case." The thought of having to squat on a German roadside while the sergeant, chaplain, and my hot husband waited in an Army-issued van sounded terrible.

Minutes later, we loaded into the van—Wilkins driving, the chaplain in the passenger seat, Noah in the front seat, and me in the row behind him.

"You can sit with me, you know," Noah said, a small smile on his face as he scooted gingerly across the seats.

I ignored the flutter in my belly at that little smile. "I know. I just thought you might need to lie down. I don't want to crowd you or make the trip any more uncomfortable than it has to be while you're still healing."

"Probably a good idea, Miller, though I can understand wanting to be near your wife after being apart." Chaplain Tate buckled his seatbelt, then angled himself so he could look back at us. "What made you decide to geo-bach?"

Noah had settled his back against the side of the van behind the driver's seat and rested his feet up on the empty bench. He glanced at me, a look full of meaning. This was our first and smallest test. Noah had used the term "geo-bach" before—it stood for geographical bachelor, as in a married soldier who lived away from his wife or family.

He winced, adjusting where he sat before speaking. "Katie was still wrappin' up school when I got orders out here, so we decided she should stay and finish. Then she got hired by a great school right off the bat, and we knew that wouldn't be easy at Kugelfels because of how small it is. It was never really the plan as much as it was... what happened."

Wilkins whistled from the driver's seat. "Man, that sucks. So you live apart, and just have to fit in visits when you can?"

I nodded, a thin smile stretching my lips, not unlike the one on Noah's face.

"Well, this will be a great time for a reunion. Terrible what happened, but it ended as well as it could. Your buddy Waverly's got a few more days of recovery, but he'll be heading home soon too." With that, the chaplain turned around and relaxed into his seat.

Captain Waverly's injuries were severe enough that I hadn't gotten to meet him. I'd hoped to, but it didn't work out due to his surgical schedule. He'd ended up having a second surgery on his fingers, from what we'd been told.

Noah rested his head against the window and shut his eyes. When he spoke, his voice sounded heavy with the need to sleep. "So, we'll get Katie settled, and then I'll check in with the unit and head to my room?"

Tate whipped around again, his eyes narrowing for just a moment before his face smoothed and he spoke. "Uh... yep. Presumably, you'll want to stay with your wife at the hotel, so we'll give you a ride back when you've got whatever you need from your place, and tomorrow or the next day, you'll start leave. We'll talk more about that with Colonel Wolfe when we get there. You guys just relax and enjoy the ride."

Noah's eyes shot to me, and my lungs locked up. Would he be spending the night in my hotel room? Of course he would. How weird and sketchy would it look if he didn't? I read it all there in his face—the apology and worry that I wasn't up for this.

"Sounds great," I scraped out, then watched the scenery streak by, my insides tying themselves in knots.

Noah

Every ounce of my self-control funneled into maintaining a calm demeanor.

"I know it's unconventional, but we'd like to pay for your convalescence," Lieutenant Colonel Wolfe—the world's most unexpectedly kind and evidently, also generous commander—spoke from where he sat at his desk in the OPFOR battalion headquarters building. "The community came together and did a fundraiser and blew it out of the water. You've got ten days, and I've booked a package at an amazing place in the Alps—just outside Garmisch. You'll have the Glockenblume hotel there and the base for fuel, plus whatever else you need at the commissary. You've been to Garmisch, right?"

I nodded, nearly struck dumb by the news. "Roger, sir. It's like heaven on earth."

LTC Wolfe's smile was small but genuine. "A perfect

description, and exactly why I chose the place. You and your wife can get some quality time there, and then you can check back in here and see how you're doing."

"Thank you, sir. That's very kind."

"Do you need to see a psych? Or have physical therapy scheduled?" He studied me, his serious face assessing my person with that sharp command he usually wore.

"No, sir. They debriefed me at Landstuhl and I'm squared away. I have calls scheduled every few days with a therapist I met with a few times there. I'm all good," I hesitated, glanced at Command Sergeant Major Allen, then added, "As far as I can tell, anyway."

Wolfe nodded slowly. "I'm glad to hear you say that. There may be things that come up as you settle in. If that happens, you tell us right away, and we deal with it then."

"Roger, sir."

"And what about your wife, Miller? Is she doing okay with all of this?" Allen's eyes narrowed.

I made a concerted effort not to shift in my seat when I thought of Katie. "Uh, yeah. I mean, obviously, it's not... how we expected to reunite, or anything."

Allen had inquired about my wife, and my marriage, several times. He was one of a small handful of people I was worried about, and the person we most had to convince since he and one other sergeant major on post had made rooting out marriage fraud their *thing*.

He studied me from where he stood next to the desk, arms crossed in his usual pose. "I can't imagine it would be, especially after so long."

Yep. They knew she'd never been to visit me, and they knew very well I hadn't been back to the States.

"Right," I agreed, knowing any disagreement would be futile, or worse, suspicious.

Allen tilted his head to one side. "So tell you what. Why don't you join up with us at the Strong Ties retreat? It starts when you're a week into your leave at the Glockenblume. That'll give you a chance to reconnect first with some alone time, then come and do some good, old-fashioned work on your marriage."

I groaned inwardly. The Strong Ties retreats were geared toward married couples and, from what I'd heard, did a great job of helping people reconnect and strengthen their marriages. They were all set in nice hotels and featured guest speakers, free books, and free hotel rooms. The ones offered at the Glockenblume, the American hotel complex nestled in the heart of Garmisch, were supposed to be especially good.

Sounded great, right? And it would be—if I were really married to my spouse. Or rather, if my spouse was actually someone I was looking to reconnect with.

"You know, Sergeant Major, that's a great idea. If you think you'll be up for it, Miller." Wolfe looked extremely pleased with the idea, which further cemented my fate.

"That sounds perfect. I'll tell Katie—she'll be thrilled."

They dismissed me, Sergeant Major's eyes gleaming with satisfaction, though I may have imagined that. LTC Wolfe shook my hand, and his heartfelt words and approach to the situation only made me admire him more than I already had, which was saying something. He told me to go home, be with my wife, and check in first thing tomorrow. That, I could do.

After changing clothes in my NCO quarters, essentially an efficiency studio apartment and nicer than any barracks I'd lived in back in the States, I walked the two blocks to the hotel. I'd spoken to my mom for a few minutes too. She'd sounded less panicked and more sure I'd be able to handle things on my own, and she didn't need to come flying in. It'd been a fight to convince her all along, but I didn't want to call any attention to the fact that Katie wasn't, and hadn't been, my primary support person in life to this point. Mom had been ecstatic to hear about the trip, which filled me with more guilt. I suspected she'd always hoped me and Katie would get together. She never pushed on that, but I hated to let her down, and combined with the feeling that I was burdening Katie, too? Brutal.

The walk to Katie's room made my leg hurt, but it felt so good to move—to just... go. I'd convinced Chaplain Tate and Sergeant Wilkins I could manage now that we'd returned to my home turf. They'd acquiesced, perhaps sensing a desire not to be babysat or treated like I needed an escort. Or maybe more so, they believed I needed this freedom after being locked in a ten-by-ten windowless room for a week.

I knocked on Katie's hotel room door at quarter to ten at night. She'd had a few days to acclimate to the time change, but I figured she'd still be awake. Plus, I needed to seem like I was at least trying to sleep with my wife after over a year apart in case someone had eyes on us. I wouldn't totally put it past Allen.

"Hey, come in." She stepped back to give me space to enter.

"You settle in okay?" I asked dumbly. Like settling in for a single night in a hotel room bordered on rocket science.

She sat on the edge of the double bed, the only offering in the small room. When I first arrived at the base, I'd spent three weeks in a room identical to this while waiting for my room in the BEQ—the Bachelor Enlisted Quarters. Since Katie didn't come with me, I didn't get housing off base. I was used to barracks living, which was easily the worst part of being a single, lower-ranking soldier, but when I moved back to the States, I'd be able to live off-base without being married.

Something about that thought soured in my stomach. But I felt like gum on the bottom of a boot at this point anyway, so it had to be due to the long day. Oh, and the whole abduction by the Taliban thing.

"Yeah. How are you? You must be exhausted."

She patted the space next to her on the bed, so I moved to sit. I'd made it a point not to get too close because having her here had proven to be a true test of will. I wanted to relax into a relationship that didn't exist. I wanted her to actually be my wife. I wanted to sit down on the bed and lay her back and welcome her, thank her, love her like I would if this were real.

Especially when she looked at me with those gentle eyes and her hair pulled back, sweatpants bunching at her ankles and a soft T-shirt looking like it was meant to be touched.

"I am about to hit the deck. I'll head back to my place, but wanted you to have this." I handed her a burner phone. "I wanted to make sure you could get ahold of me."

One small part of being kidnapped by terrorists? They took all my gear. Everything. They left me and Waverly in our boxer briefs and T-shirts. They took every other part of our uniforms—boots, weapons, dog tags, the photos in our pockets, our cell phones. Luckily, we'd left our wallets and personal phones at the base, so the guys who didn't get captured and later medically transported out of the country, had taken the things back to Germany with them. Lieutenant Colonel Wolfe had gifted me the phone and a few other things—my packed uniforms and other clothes—at our meeting.

"Oh, thanks. I figured I'd just use Wi-Fi whenever I could, but this'll help." She turned the small phone over in her hand.

"I know it's basic, but at least you can make a call if you need me. I don't want you to feel even more isolated than you probably do." I swallowed down a welling of guilt and regret that she'd upended her life to come be with me.

"Thank you. That was thoughtful."

We sat quietly on the bed, no sounds in the room but the ticking of a radiator down the hallway. I wanted to collapse back on the bed and pull her close. Maybe fall asleep smelling her hair and feeling her T-shirt, her soft body next to mine.

Not an option, though. Probably not a great idea to let the imagination run wild—I'd been without a woman for years, and I'd just come out of a crazy situation. Dr. Wagner had already warned me about heightened emotions. Obviously, they'd come to play tonight.

I stood. "I'll head out now and check in tomorrow. My commander is a crazy person and arranged for us to go on a little vacation, so we'll leave then. I know we have a lot to talk about, but at least you'll get to see some of Germany while you're here."

Her eyes lit with excitement, and she walked the whopping five feet with me to the door. "That's amazing. Thank you."

A humorless chuckle escaped, and then I winced at the resulting twinge in my sore ribs. "I'm not sure you'll be thankin' me when all is said and done, but we'll make the best of it."

Our gazes locked, and her light brown eyes gave me a tilting sense of vertigo before she set a hand on my arm. "You know, Noah, I know we don't know each other all that well, but I'm glad to be here. It's terrible circumstances, but I don't want you to keep apologizing, okay?"

I nodded.

She leaned in close, and my feeble heart skyrocketed into action, pumping with gusto at her nearness. Good grief, she smelled good—sweet and warm. Just... feminine and lovely. I bet if I kissed her neck, it'd taste just the same.

"Get some sleep."

Her breath brushed my ear, and I fought a shiver. Then she kissed my cheek, her perfect lips gentle and maddening at my skin.

If I spoke then, my voice would've betrayed me. It would've revealed my ragged wanting of her, so inappropriate *now*. And after all this time, so out of place and unwelcome. So instead, I nodded, a thin smile smeared on my face, and left.

The door shut behind me and I let out a long exhale, wishing... Well, just wishing.

CHAPTER FIVE

Katie

Noah looked so tired, I couldn't believe he could still stand. Add to it he had some pretty intense injuries he was dealing with, and I couldn't imagine how he'd walked home. I fretted over him getting back safely and finally gave in to the need to check on him by text. I used the new little phone he'd bought me. It felt like a blast from the past because it wasn't a smartphone, but it did the trick.

His response that he'd made it back eased my worry, though I didn't sleep any better than I had since that very first knock on my door. Had it really been less than two weeks ago?

I woke ready for whatever came my way, somehow feeling bold and confident in my role to help Noah more than I ever would've expected. Certainly, I wasn't confident in my role as his *wife*. But if we were heading out on vacation, I wouldn't need to do much pretending, and maybe I'd make it home before we were put too much to the test. Then things could naturally unwind while I returned stateside, and when he filed for divorce, no one would question him. Maybe we could even stage a fight before I left.

That'd be good—a real end to things. I'd move past this years-long infatuation, and we'd remain distant friends. I'd pick up whatever pieces cracked and crumbled off my heart in the process, and I *would* be fine. So would he.

Soon, I'd begin my master's program and see what life felt like as an unmarried woman. Excitement and not a little dread swirled in my belly. A lot to look forward to, and a lot of change all at once. It'd be fine.

My stomach cramped, and I wondered if I was dehydrated, which led me to guzzle some water before finishing up the last of my makeup. I wore just enough to look pretty, I hoped, but not enough to have to really deal with it. A little powder, mascara, and Chapstick, and I was ready to go. I'd learned to keep my morning routine simple because the total obliterating kind of tiredness that ensued at the beginning of each school year demanded simplicity in the mornings.

A pang of missing my kids shot through me. The kindergarteners in my class this year, like every year, had my heart. I'd been gone for a week and a half, though I barely remembered those couple days after they told me Noah'd been taken. I'd tried to work the first few days, but I was a wreck and no good to the kids or anyone else, so they'd gently suggested I start leave.

I hopped on my laptop and sent an e-mail to my long-term substitute, checking in. My principal had been so understanding and helpful, and I'd been given amazing flexibility. I also knew my sub and she was awesome, so my kids were in good hands. Still, I missed them, and the guilt of not being there nagged at me, even though I knew I'd done the right thing by coming. Maybe a bit of that guilt also hung on me as my regular teaching came to an end.

Should I consider it a failure that I'd only gotten two years into teaching before abandoning ship? It wasn't that I didn't love the kids. And my principal was amazing. But she was the reason I saw my skills were better suited to administration. I'd considered it in undergrad but felt sure I was wrong, only to see with startling clarity how much I wanted to transition to the admin side—the dark side, as my friend Sarah had joked.

I shook off those thoughts, returning my focus to sending the e-mail, then gathering up the last few straggling things, my mind jumping from thought to thought all the while.

What would've happened if I hadn't come? Would Mrs. Miller, Noah's mom, have come? We hadn't discussed that. And what an odd thought, since technically I *was* Mrs. Miller. Even my kids called me Mrs. Miller at school. But in my mind, I just felt like... Katie. Just Katie.

Noah and Mrs. Miller, the original, were close. She and I talked occasionally, even still, but I didn't know if she could leave the farm this time of year. I mean, of course she would in these circumstances, and come to think of it, maybe she would still come? I didn't know that either.

A knock thudded at the door and I jumped, my nerves still wrapped tight from the intensity of the last few weeks.

"Hey, darlin'. Did you sleep?" Noah stood tall and muscular and entirely inaccessible to me just outside my door, a half-smile on his face. That accent and the low timbre of his voice should've necessitated a cowboy hat and tight Wranglers.

The man had the whole Southern rugged charm thing

going on. I'd liked that about him the moment I met him, especially since his accent had seemed novel after moving from Idaho to Kansas and finally landing in Kentucky. But then again, I'd hardly talked to anyone at that point, nor would I for another few weeks before my stepfather unlocked my door again.

But that's another story for another day.

"Not much, but that's okay." I grabbed my bag and purse.

When I turned to face him again, I caught his eyes wandering over me before they met mine again. He cleared his throat and frowned. "Me neither."

Something low in my belly fluttered at how he'd looked at me like that—with interest. That level of perusal was something new between us. He'd never, not a single time, showed any interest in me physically. He'd been very clear when we sat in the living room at his mother's farmhouse, that he expected nothing from me in that way. And at the time, it'd been a relief. Only a small, distant twinge of hurt had struck at the thought that he didn't find me attractive, but I knew it was for the best.

I was eighteen and he was twenty-one. I'd been isolated for most of my adolescent years, and my escape to the court-house the day I became legal had been the most terrifying and exhilarating hours of my life.

I married the most handsome man I'd ever seen—the isolation might've made that less impressive, but I could honestly say it remained true. We drove to the military base where he was stationed hours away from the house that'd never been a home for me, and he'd put me up in the hotel before returning to his barracks. I'd never stayed in a hotel, so even the on-base military lodging had made me feel free and grown. And like I could breathe.

The security gate a street or two over that required a military ID for entrance definitely helped with that feeling, too.

Blinking back to the present, I shut the door to the military lodging hotel here and now and followed the slightly hunched bulk of my husband down a pathway to a small black car.

"This is me. I already checked you out at Reception."

He held out a hand for my bag, which I gave him, then realized what I'd done and pulled it back. "Don't be crazy," I muttered, annoyed with myself for automatically handing him the bag when he'd been injured.

He shrugged, then opened the passenger side door before moving to pop the trunk. I slid the suitcase into the space before he closed it, ducked into the passenger seat, and shut the door. Then I watched in amazement as he folded himself into the tiny car. Even at his height, he looked completely comfortable, though the driver's seat was pushed back almost to the bench of the back passenger's spot.

"It's not glamorous, but it'll get us where we need to go safely. Germans don't do big beefy trucks or giant SUVs, and gas is expensive even with the rations the Army gives us." His cheeks colored like he was embarrassed.

My stomach dipped at his blush. He was too adorable, and piling that on top of how aggressively handsome he was put me in serious trouble. "This is great. I'm just amazed you fit. I guess this means you'd fit in my Prius back home."

He chuckled. "Guess so."

He notched the gear shift into place and eased backward, then moved us onto the street I vaguely recognized as the main drag of the small Army post. I'd been on exactly two military bases before—Fort Campbell and Fort Bragg.

Campbell was big but manageable, and once I saw Fort Bragg, I said a prayer of thanks that it hadn't been my first experience with a military base. The place literally had its own highway rolling through it. In no way did overwhelming sufficiently describe it.

We drove for a minute or two, him pointing out the clinic, the library, the street that would lead toward the commissary, and the long road that wound around to the post office. Then we parked and he twisted in his seat to face me.

He frowned slightly. "So, this has the potential to be a lot, but we've got to stop in here before we get goin'. I have no way to prepare you for any of this except to say most of these people are my friends. They're here to celebrate that I didn't get offed by the bad guys, and they're all a little overeager to meet you."

My eyes must've grown two sizes as I stared at him, dread dropping like a too-big barbell in my stomach. "Oh."

He reached over and set a hand on mine where it rested on my thigh. "This will be fine, Katie. They'll be nice and excited, and if you ever don't know what to do, just come get me or ask a question. They know we've lived apart, and they know you don't have much experience with the Army life, so no one will expect you to talk the talk."

Some other uncomfortable sensation pierced my chest at that. I'd been almost wholly removed, except for our occasional messages and e-mails. I'd never wanted to keep my distance so much, but he'd always been so careful not to bother me, and I'd gotten the message. I didn't want to pester him with constant updates and interrupt his life.

"Okay. I can do that."

His bright blue eyes softened, and he set a hand on the back of my neck, then ducked his head so our faces were inches apart, effectively sending my heart into overdrive. "I owe you everything and I know that. I'm hopin' the next week is going to make up for some of the madness you're starin' down."

"You do not owe me." I summoned a weak smile, my insides roiling with dread and nerves. And maybe even a little swoon at his words and the touch of his hand on my skin. I had no way to handle this other than just to wade in. "Let's do it."

He led the way, my hand in his, into a building with a large sign that looked like a restaurant or bar called The Place. Upon entering, a big cheer went up and about twenty faces applauded as we wandered in.

Noah pulled me close and wrapped an arm around my waist, then dropped a kiss on my forehead that I couldn't even think about because there was just no time. I'd save the memory for later—that and the handholding, and the arm around my waist. And his clean laundry scent I wanted to curl up in.

"Thanks for comin', y'all."

Somehow, that simple phrase caused the small crowd to erupt again. Cheers, whistles, whoops, and claps clanged around us so loudly I would've expected the sound to be coming from a group two times the size.

"This is my wife. Please be gentle with her. She's had a rough few weeks."

Then he turned me to him and kissed my cheek and hugged me so tight it must have crushed his ribs. The air went out of me so fast I thought I'd never find it again.

CHAPTER SIX

Noah

Ibattled with myself about the physical contact.

I'd kissed her forehead and her cheek. And, sweet tea on a Sunday, did I want to kiss those lips. But we'd touched more in the last twenty minutes than we had in the entirety of our relationship. Me touching the nape of her neck, holding her hand, hugging her... It was all new territory.

I'd pecked her cheek at the courthouse because it had felt odd not to kiss her in some way, but kissing her lips would've been too much. She was literally fleeing her family, and though we'd technically been neighbors for two years, I had hardly been there. Plus, even if I had—from what my mom told me and part of why she'd gotten to know what was going on with Katie in the first place—I wouldn't have seen her anyway.

Her family had locked her in her room with a deadbolt

lock on her door that she didn't have a key to. And maybe by *family*, I should specify it was her stepfather and step-brother because her mom was so high out of her mind she had no idea what was going on. It was astounding she hadn't been abused more than that, though sometimes I wondered if she had been, and she'd never told my mom. She and I hadn't talked about it. I'd asked a few times those first few months, but she'd taken her troubles to a therapist and that person had far more skill to help her than I did.

"You said she was beautiful, man, but I had no idea." Captain Thatcher Wild shook my hand and jolted me from my memories. Probably best to stay tuned in to the present after all.

"I said very clearly she's the prettiest girl I've ever seen," I defended, squeezing her closer. That was true—both that I'd described Katie that way, and that I thought she was. It wasn't even a thought; it was fact.

"Thatcher Wild, ma'am. So glad your man's back, and so happy to meet you." Wild held out his hand to Katie, which she took and shook briefly.

Not a flinch or anything. She used to shrink into herself. Of course, it'd been years since I'd had to introduce her to anyone. And the last time, it had just been to the lawyer to get our documents organized for my deployment. But still, she'd gained confidence or lost some of that nagging fear—or maybe both.

"You must be Katie. I'm so glad you're here." A small blond woman pulled Katie into her arms. "I'm Livie. I'm not even officially a military spouse yet, but I just want to say *welcome*. I'm so happy to meet you."

I eyed her, then pulled it together when I saw Lieu-tenant Colonel Wolfe approach behind her. He held out a hand, which I shook.

"Livie is my fiancée," he explained.

"Congratulations, sir. That's great news. And nice to meet you, ma'am." I nodded to her but settled my arm back around Katie. Something made me want to keep her attached to me, which I decided wasn't a bad impulse. If she were really my wife, I'd feel that way too. Plus, she had no idea who these people were, so it seemed only fair to provide her a tether.

"It's so nice to meet you, Noah. Eric's been so worried. I'm glad you're back safe."

Livie's sincerity shone through her eyes, and I could see how well she fit with Lieutenant Colonel Wolfe. I had no idea he'd gotten engaged, but good for him. He was a good man and deserved someone awesome.

They wandered away and more people circulated through—Sergeant Major Allen, David Reyes, Masters, other officers, and quite a few NCOs from the battalion. They'd do something official for us after leave, probably, but it was nice of all these guys to come. Granted, they might've just come for the free food. There was a catered setup with meats and cheeses, semmel rolls, various cheese spreads and pretzels, and a large sheet cake. Something about Army get-togethers made people want sheet cake, even at ten a.m.

I ducked my head, steering us over to the food table after chatting with Emily Wender, the head of the Education Center, who I'd gotten to know while taking courses there. Then Major Reynolds headed us off just before we got to the setup.

"Nothing like celebrating your return from capture with a sheet cake, right, Miller?"

Major Reynolds held out a hand and I shook it. I'd seen him just last night, but the man was congenial as all get out, so no surprise he'd come to greet me here.

"No, sir. Can you mark any occasion in the Army without one?"

We chuckled, and then I urged Katie forward. "This is my wife, Katie Miller."

Lord, I wouldn't tire of saying that, even if it made me stupid to admit it.

"Very nice to meet you, ma'am." Reynolds flashed one of his lady-killer smiles.

I might've gotten a little jealous at the way she blushed when she shook his hand, but he was all right. He just had that way about him—all likable and pretty and charming, the jerk.

"Well, sir, we're going to grab some food," I said, arm back around Katie.

He gestured grandly toward the table next to him. "Please do. Enjoy."

I picked up a plate and held one out for Katie.

"How are you holdin' up?"

She laughed a little. "I'm good. Though I am hungry, so this is great. Thank you."

We inched along, selecting our food, then sat across from each other at a table.

"So, Katie. Are you looking forward to the Strong Ties retreat?" Sergeant Major Allen spoke where he stood just behind me.

"Uh, pardon?" She covered her mouth for a moment as she chewed, then dropped her hand, but I spoke first.

"We're excited, yes, Sergeant Major. Thanks for thinkin' of it. Will we see you and Mrs. Allen there?" I slid sideways on the bench so I could turn enough to see him.

"Absolutely."

"Well, that's great. I'm sure Katie will look forward to meetin' her." I smiled encouragingly at Katie, praying she wouldn't ask questions and that Allen would take the hint and leave us alone.

"I can't wait," she said, smiling brightly back at me and Allen.

After what felt like hours, but was really only another thirty-five minutes or so, Katie and I waved goodbye to the group of well-wishers and hustled off to the car. I had the odd thought that it felt like we were leaving a wedding reception and heading out on our honeymoon when all our friends waved at us driving away.

Except they were only my friends, she'd just barely met them, and we'd been married for coming up on five years. And we'd definitely never had a honeymoon. Or a wedding night, even.

I exhaled sharply, pushing away those thoughts. They weren't productive, especially now that we were back in the car and back to just the two of us, heading out on a ten-day vacation where we'd be alone for the first seven days, then on to a marriage retreat. It would effectively multiply the time we'd spent together, much less together *alone*, exponentially.

So, thinking of honeymoons was not productive. Or perhaps it was *too* productive, my imagination more than ready to supply possibilities for our upcoming stay in the mountains. It had to come from all these years with no one. The last time I'd had a girlfriend, I'd been twenty.

"Thanks for hangin' in there with me. We have a ton to talk about, and I'm sorry I caught you off guard. They only called me about that this morning. I didn't feel like I could say no. Might be why they waited till the last minute and didn't tell me last night." In fact, I knew it was. If they'd told me even last night, I might've backed out and not felt too bad, but this morning had left me with no options.

They knew I couldn't back out an hour before the thing started.

"It was so nice of them. You have some great friends here." Her gaze focused out the window, taking in the tree-lined road while we drove, but her voice had a wistful quality to it.

"I do. Most of them are work buddies, and then obviously you met Colonel Wolfe, the battalion commander."

She hummed at that. "He was always nice. He called every day to check in with me."

A cold feeling sank in my gut. She meant while they held me captive. "I'm glad. He's a good commander."

"I could tell. I mean, not that I know, but he seemed thoughtful, and he handled me and my hysteria well." She chuckled, but it sounded forced.

I wished I could reach out and hold her hand, try to provide comfort. But my manual transmission wouldn't allow for that while I navigated a neighborhood on the way to the autobahn. Not yet, anyway. I hoped the next few days could help. I'd always found comfort in nature, and we were heading to the heart of natural beauty.

"I'm sorry you've had to deal with this. I—"

Her hand on my leg stopped me.

"Noah, please. Stop apologizing. We're about to head into the Alps. I'm in Europe for the first time in my life, and I want to just... be here. Okay?"

I glanced at her, then back to the road. She seemed to mean it, and I thanked God for that. But I needed her to know that our time in the mountains wouldn't be all fun and games.

"About the trip—we're doing the first seven at the resort, and then we're going to be joining the battalion's Strong Ties retreat."

"You mentioned that, but what is it exactly?"

I let out a sigh, wishing I didn't feel like we had to do this. But we did.

"It's a marriage retreat. The Army pays for our stay in a fancy hotel, and a chaplain will lead discussion or whatever. I honestly don't know the ins and outs since I haven't been to one, obviously. Sergeant Major Allen suggested we go since the unit's retreat lines up perfectly with the last few days of our trip, and we're already there. I couldn't think of a way to get out of it or I would have."

I couldn't look at her to gauge her response, which drove me insane. The three-hour drive to our destination would be painful if she kept all her words so close.

"We'll be fine. Thankfully, it's at the end of the trip, not the beginning. We've got a week to get to know each other and learn enough to convince your bosses we've been together for years."

I let her words and confidence soak in, willing it to be true.

Katie

My eyes shot open and surveyed my surroundings, then I exhaled in relief. I'd dreamed of my step-brother, standing over me with a cigarette, threatening that if I talked back to him or his father, he'd put it out on my face. It was a familiar scene from my childhood and just one of the many reasons I'd fled.

Happily, I woke to Noah swiping through his phone, evidently searching for something. His head bowed over the device, a small frown on his masculine face. Mm, he was hand-some, and seeing him so close made my chest flutter. I shifted in the seat, wondering when I'd fallen asleep. It must've been a while ago because I didn't remember much of the drive.

"Sorry I passed out on you," I said, arching my back to ease the ache there.

He glanced over, then averted his eyes back to his phone

and cleared his throat. "No problem. You're still jet lagged, I'm sure. I'm glad you could rest."

I surveyed the scene out the window... *wow*. Vast mountains crested ahead of us, covered in thick greenery and craggy rocks in places, particularly toward the top. I could see a few different towers that at first looked like telephone poles. But after closer inspection, little chairs became visible, which meant they had to be ski lifts. I'd never been to a ski resort.

"Ah, there it is," Noah said, quiet enough it seemed to be for his ears only.

"What'd you lose?"

"I couldn't find the confirmation Colonel Wolfe forwarded me. No idea why that was so difficult. But now we're good to go—let's check-in."

We left our bags in the car for the time being and crossed the cobblestone circular entrance into a lobby that was so lovely, I gasped, and for some reason, grabbed Noah's hand. My eyes wandered from the stone fireplace that filled the two-story room at the far end, to the over-sized curved-back chairs big enough for two or more. They looked cushy and after the long car ride, I could've sunk into one and stayed a while.

I admired the cream, gray, and natural wood color scheme. It looked fresh and clean, especially with boxes of long grasses creating a whole wall of bright green behind the reception desk.

My eyes flitted from one thing to the next; there were so many details to take in. This was nothing like an American hotel or at least nothing like any I'd stayed in. I'd only been in a handful since I'd left my old life behind—mostly military lodging, a few Holiday Inn Expresses, and one

Hampton Inn when I'd splurged on a post-graduation weekend away with a friend.

We slowed to a stop in front of a smiling woman, complete with what I gathered was a traditional German dress and a crown woven of her own braid at her brow. Then I realized I was still holding Noah's hand, and heat flew to my cheeks as I dropped it.

"Sorry," I whispered.

He set a hand on my back to reassure me, or maybe just to look husbandly when he spoke, effectively silencing me and sending tendrils of heat in all directions from the place where he touched me.

"Ah, Mr. and Mrs. Miller. Very happy to welcome you for your stay." The woman's English was perfectly crisp and clear. It contrasted starkly to Noah's low, draggy Southern accent, but I loved hearing both.

Had anyone called us *Mr. and Mrs. Miller* before? Was it crazy that hearing that as he stood with his hand on me made my stomach drop through the floor and simultaneously feel like I was floating? It sounded... *good.*

She maneuvered through rapid typing, selecting keys—real, actual metal keys—and then set a giant reusable bag branded with the hotel's logo stuffed with welcome gifts on the counter. "Daniel, would you show the Millers to their room, please?"

Daniel appeared behind us, tall and thin as a rail and looking about eighteen. "Do you have baggage?"

"We left it in the car." Noah made a regretful face.

Daniel bowed just an inch in acknowledgment. "If you would like me to take the car and park it below, I can retrieve the bags when I return."

Okay, wow. Super fancy. Not only would they park the car, but they'd also get the bags? If I didn't know Noah's car was spotless and his trunk held nothing beyond a little safety kit and a snow scraper, I'd be worried. But Daniel would have no trouble figuring out what belonged in the room.

I wished, not for the first time, I had a less trashed suitcase. Maybe I'd treat myself to a nice one when I returned from all this. I hoped Noah wasn't embarrassed.

We followed Daniel up a carpeted ramp and through a large sitting area that was attached to a gorgeous all-wood bar. We passed what looked like the entrance to a formal dining room, and then a door that said *Schwimbad. Huh.* I really wished I had German knowledge, though *schwim* seemed promisingly like it might have to do with a pool.

We continued on around a corner, and I could hardly take in everything at once—the strategic little places where guests could stop and sit. The wall of windows looking out at the towering mountains. A double-doorway to what looked like another dining room.

Anxiety tightened in my belly as I realized how much this must be costing Noah. I couldn't imagine he could afford this. He'd said his friends had footed the bill, but we'd still need to eat. Would they charge for every bottle of water, every snack, every time we sat on one of the gorgeous chaise lounges I could see out the window?

I had some savings, but I'd been saving for years so I could afford an apartment without issue once the divorce came through. I had financial aid for the master's program, and I could always get something part-time if I needed extra income. But I needed a cushion and the security of knowing I had one even if I lost my job. I had to know I would never have a circumstance that drove me back to the place I'd left.

Not that anything could cause that. I'd live on the streets before I went back—if they were even still there.

All of that to say, I could put money toward this. I'd calculated what I had to spend before I'd flown out—one of many things I'd struggled to focus on while waiting to hear that Noah had been found. More than anything, I didn't want to be a burden to him in yet another way.

"Please, just call reception if you need anything. *Kaffe und Kuchen* begins in only an hour and one half, and dinner service begins at half-six. Enjoy your stay." Daniel bowed slightly, his go-to move, then spun on his heel and disappeared out the door which shut behind him with a thud.

I'd been so preoccupied with thoughts of the expense of the place, I hadn't absorbed the room while following Daniel in his dark brown suit.

"This'll do," Noah said, a smile brightening his voice. He looked at me with a big grin.

"Yeah, it's decent."

We chuckled at the understatement because this place screamed luxury. The door opened to a wall lined with wood, then jutted into what I could only describe as a little nest—a nook made for cuddling up and reading with soft seating and piles of fluffy pillows and a cozy throw blanket in a muted gray.

A glass table with two chairs so sleek and delicate I'd be nervous to sit on them was situated just in front of the glass doors that led to a balcony. I assumed it would be another fantastic view. At present, gauzy sheets billowed with a breeze that came through the door.

And then... a bed. A huge, gorgeous bed set low to the ground with comforters that had to be a foot thick and so fluffy, one on each half of the bed. Three perfectly plumped pillows lined up neatly at the headboard, and white sheets showed under the comforters.

"I want to dive into that and never come out," I said with a sigh.

"Yep." Noah's response came out strangled, but when I looked at him, he shifted to wander around the other side of the bed.

"Oh, wow."

I shuffled over to see and giggled. I'd never imagined a bathroom so ridiculously over the top. They did the entire thing in a light gray granite, glass, and white porcelain. There were white towels and bright, warm lights.

To the left, a long glass panel shielded a space with floor-to-ceiling light blue tiles that matched the granite somehow. There was also one of those huge rain shower heads the size of a car tire with an opening at the far end, but no door.

Oh. No barrier between the room itself and the bathroom either, for that matter. There was just a small hallway with a bend in it which would, in theory, keep cooler air out or in. Mercifully, there did seem to be a rather sturdy door on the room to the toilet. The focal point of the bathroom, though, was the enormous tub. It truly looked the size of a hot tub and had little holes all along the base and sides that must've been for air jets.

Hello there. I'd have to figure out a way to experience that at least once. I could imagine relaxing in a giant bubble bath, and there'd be enough room for Noah—

Whoooa. Better settle that right down.

Speaking of, Noah had left me to my musings and the blush climbing to my cheeks at the thoughts of the tub and its many uses. I turned to the sinks—two large, rectangular porcelain basins set inside a granite countertop, tall faucets arching over each. The entire wall other than the sink itself held a mirror that served to make the bathroom look gigantic. It also guaranteed no privacy. My stomach flipped at the reality that we'd be sharing this space, all the opulence and comfort—for days. And nights.

We'd figure it out.

I unwrapped a small soap and set it on the grooved part of the counter clearly meant for the job, then washed my hands. I didn't need to, though it never hurt, but I needed something to do with myself. When I emerged from the bathroom, Noah was receiving our bags from Daniel, who must've teleported himself around in order to get them to us so quickly.

"That was insanely fast," I said, grabbing my gargantuan beast.

"It was. I tried to tip him but he refused. I forgot they don't do tips like that here." He shot me a fake embarrassed look.

"Wait, they don't? Like... at all?" This seemed like essential information for meals, too.

"Tipping in Europe is very different. Depends on where you are, but here, they don't tip except for at meals. And even then, it's usually like a euro per person, even for fancy meals. It feels strange to go out and have a nice meal and leave what amounts to only a few dollars for a tip." He turned and busied himself with putting his bag on a table-like section of the closet and unloading his clothes.

"That's awesome, but also would be strange. Help me remember so I don't make a fool of myself," I said.

"Well, we won't have to do much of that at all here—it's all-inclusive." He turned with a bright smile.

"Really? Like all meals or just breakfast like they do in the States some places?"

He chuckled low. "Not just a crappy microwaved omelet or stale toast, I'm guessin'. I looked at the photos on their website last night before I passed out, and I think we're going to eat well. The only thing is..." A frown wrinkled his brow.

I raised mine, waiting, eager for whatever he had to say. That could arguably be my perpetual state—willing to take anything he'd give.

"Well, since it's all-inclusive, it seems like they might expect us to eat together. They'll seat us at the same table for each meal and stuff like that. I don't want you to feel like you have to eat with me for every meal, so we can figure that out, but—"

I moved to him and set a hand on his wrist to still him, the boldness to touch him rooted in his contact with me earlier at the gathering with his friends. Still, the feel of his warmth, a dusting of blond hair against his tanned skin, made my stomach clench. "You're the only person I know here, Noah. I definitely want to eat with you."

He swallowed and it looked like it took effort.

"Okay." His eyes flickered over my shoulder, then returned to meet mine again. "Then, while we're at it, I guess we should talk about where we're goin' to sleep."

CHAPTER EIGHT

Noah

I'd swear her eyes got larger at that. Her cheeks already seemed pink, but the color deepened, and the stretch of her exposed chest where the vee of her T-shirt dipped all the way up onto her throat reddened too. I didn't mean to embarrass her, but we needed to address it before we were both even more tired and ready to sleep. I'd assumed there'd be a couch, but there was just a little reading nook.

"You know what, we don't need to discuss it. I sleep curled up anyway—I can take the little spot over there." I nodded to the cushy space. It really did look comfortable.

Though, let's be real. I'd one hundred percent rather sleep in the bed next to her.

"No way. If anyone's sleeping there, it's me." She crossed the room and took a seat, then leaned over to rest her head on a pillow. "See? Perfect."

I shook my head, moving over to her and ignoring how

inviting she made the little space look just by being in it. "Not a chance. I'm sleepin' there. You're the guest here, and I want you to have a great time."

She stared at me, nearly to the point of glaring. Her lips pursed just slightly, but after a moment, she relented. "Fine. I can tell you're not going to give up on this, so you take it tonight and we'll see how it goes."

She did it again—the thing she always did. She looked up at me kind of... adoringly. And like *I* always did, at least lately, I thought about how I wished I could kiss her. Maybe slide her further into the little nest and get comfortable together.

But it wasn't an option, and I'd need to keep that under wraps. I cleared my throat again, probably for the tenth time since we'd arrived. "I'm going to go explore a bit. Why don't you get unpacked? I'll swing back around and pick you up so we can go check out the *Kaffe und Kuchen* setup."

"That's like a coffee hour, I guess?" she asked, peeling herself off the cozy spot.

"Yeah. It's coffee and cake—usually like late afternoon into early evening. I'm surprised their dinner hour starts so early, but that's nice. I'm guessin' we'll want to hit the hay pretty early tonight."

Something hungry twisted low in my gut. I mentally told my gut to shut the hell up. I couldn't be having a reaction every damn time I talked about going to bed, or this week would be even longer than I could've imagined.

"Sounds perfect. I'll be here."

She smiled, unzipping her suitcase, and something thumped in my chest. I grabbed a key and left without looking back because I was seriously worried about the consequences of letting myself look at her for too long.

How had I managed to marry a woman I'd be so

intensely attracted to? I mean, considering it was a sham marriage. I'd married her to genuinely help her out, knowing I'd get a little financial kickback, too. But more than anything, I'd felt truly scared for her once my mom started telling me about things she'd seen. Katie'd been pretty then, of course, but young and sad and broken on a few levels. She'd never been *mine*, and I'd known she never would be.

I internally scoffed at myself. That was a load. I'd had a crush on her the minute I saw her. She was completely beautiful then, and if her stepfather hadn't interrupted us, I probably would've asked her out. Not that I'd ever been grateful to that bastard for anything, but it was only later that I found out she was sixteen and probably not someone I should start something up with.

I'd wanted to help her, but the impulse to say yes without thinking? That'd come from the Noah of old, who'd not gotten her out of his head no matter how many times he'd tried.

The last few times I'd seen her in our post-marriage years, I'd appreciated her beauty. Especially in the absence of the darkness that had so often shadowed her in those first few days, and even years, when we'd interacted. Damn, she was strikingly gorgeous and had only grown more so. But after we married, it hadn't seemed right to... want her. And I'd tried not to, even to the point of avoiding her. Would've been a waste of energy, anyway.

And the same could be said now. We were a little over two months away from what would've been the end of it all. *Or, what will be the end of it all,* I reminded myself.

I wandered the hotel, only half-seeing things despite the incredible beauty, the woman back in the room occupying my thoughts even in the face of the Alpine heights and amazing hotel features. Maybe we could tour around together after a snack.

I burned an hour walking aimlessly and returned no closer to clearheaded than when I'd left. But I'd resolved to enjoy the trip—focus on relaxing away from work, making sure my mind was right after the ordeal in Afghanistan, and enjoying time with Katie as a last hurrah. That it was also essentially our first didn't need to factor in.

I slid my key in the lock, then paused, wondering if I should knock, just in case. I pulled the key out and pocketed it, suddenly embarrassed by the impulse to just barge in.

I knocked and waited, knocked and waited, checked my phone, and finally decided maybe she'd left to do some exploring of her own. I opened the door carefully, not sure what I expected, but I just didn't want to kick things off on the wrong foot. Or, any more wrong than forcing a woman you hardly knew and were about to divorce into traveling across the world after taking a leave of absence from work to pick up your busted butt from a hospital.

"Katie?" I hollered ahead, but no answer. Glancing around, I could see nothing out of place, and her suitcase must've been tucked away in the closet because it was now gone. Then I noticed the breeze blowing through the curtains and the door standing wide. I could make out her silhouette outside.

"Incredible view," I said quietly, stepping out to join her. She jumped, but only a little.

The balcony overlooked a bit of the property, then a long, grassy valley stretched out until the Zugspitze—the tallest mountain in Germany—and its fellows jutted out of the ground and pierced the sky. That, at least the tallest point, was technically Germany, though we could see it since we were in a town just over the Austrian border. To the right was another peak, much closer and less impressive than the giants at a distance, but still imposing and shouting its beauty.

"I can't stop looking. It's like my lungs can expand more fully here or something. Though that doesn't make sense because aren't we at a higher altitude?" She chuckled and turned to me, and I stifled a gasp.

She had an easy smile, biting her lip with that little hint of self-deprecation. She'd taken her hair from the ponytail she'd worn it in earlier and spiraled and flipped around her face until it rested on her shoulders. She'd changed into a different shirt—a powder blue, silky-looking thing that draped a little around her neck and showed off a small necklace at her collarbone.

"I changed my top. I wasn't sure if we should be more... dressy, maybe? Everything is so perfect here, it seems weird to bum around in jeans and a T-shirt." She leaned her back against the railing, which I noticed butted up against window boxes full of pansies and geraniums, somehow gloriously in bloom despite it only being the very beginning of May.

She fit perfectly there, standing in front of the mountains and the bright little red and pink flowers—just so damn beautiful. Like God was saying, *look what I can do* all in one snapshot.

"You look—" Unexpectedly, the words caught in my throat. I would end up having to run away from her constantly if I couldn't at least *talk* to her.

Get it together, man.

"You're gorgeous, Katie. No matter what you wear."

Her lashes fluttered and she smiled, but it wasn't full—it was quieter, maybe a little unsure or shy. "Thank you. You are too."

I let out a puff of air that sounded like *hah* and ran a hand over my head through the hair that'd gotten a little long on top. "Thanks. Let's go check out the set-up for this snack time, huh?"

I brushed off the impulse to hold out a hand. Instead, I tucked them both into my pockets and stepped back inside.

We found our way to the dining area for the snack time meal, an all-wood, rustic-style lodge that looked right out of a ski movie. Even in late spring, it held so much charm and made me wish we'd come in winter. The carved wooden booth with cushions for comfort made the meal comfortable and easy. We chose our food from a surprisingly full buffet that featured two kinds of soup, a small salad bar, a variety of pickled vegetables, a selection of cured meats and cheeses, semmel rolls and a large loaf of multi-grain bread, and two different desserts—a cherry tart and a creamy vanilla layer cake.

"This is insane, right? This is a huge meal." Katie smiled over her plate, which I happily noticed had been filled to bursting, and beside it sat a little soup bowl full of creamy corn chowder.

"It is. I'd think this was lunch if I didn't know for a fact this is somethin' different. We better be careful or we'll never have room for dinner." I sipped a cappuccino which felt like such a vacation thing. I only ever drank black coffee out of habit and necessity, so anything fancier felt totally separate from my real life.

Might as well. This whole thing was like one giant dream—one that came after a long, waking nightmare.

Waverly and I had talked about coffee—our favorites, the worst cup we'd ever had, all that. We'd talked about almost everything in the course of our week together. But damn, I didn't want to be thinking of that now when Katie sat across from me, beautiful and smiling and triumphant over her own past. I shouldered the thoughts away, determined not to get dragged into the flashes of memory that would come if I didn't resist.

We ate and chatted, and had moments of silence where we both just sat and people-watched. We heard Italian, lots of German, two different British accents, and something else we couldn't identify because the people were so quiet.

"I think we're the only Americans," she said, something sparkling in her eye.

"Why do I feel like that's makin' you really happy?"

Her smile widened. "I don't know, but it does. It feels more... authentic. I don't know. That's dumb, but I like it being just you and me."

I like it being just you and me.

I did too. Already. I'd even liked the drive up while she slept, listening to her breathing, her body curled up in the seat and head resting against the car door. So far, I liked everything about her. She had flaws and baggage like anyone, and I only knew a little about her history, but I'd evidently lost the ability to see anything but how amazing she was.

Crap timing, what with the divorce coming up and all.

CHAPTER NINE

Katie

We'd stayed until everyone else in the rustic lodge eating area had left, lingering over one last helping of the soup I wanted to eat every day for the rest of my life. Our conversation came surprisingly easy for two people who didn't know each other and only ever talked business.

That, too, had my heart skipping around making eyes at him.

By the time we returned to the room after a slow wander around the resort, he was limping slightly and I felt dead on my feet. I should've already adjusted to the jet lag, and I thought I was, but I hadn't actually slept much—never more than four hours at a time—since arriving four nights ago.

When he asked if I minded if he called it a night, I sighed with relief and said it sounded perfect. We took turns readying for bed in the bathroom. He walked out a few minutes after entering, and I'd already jumped under the covers.

"There's no way you can stretch out your leg well enough over there. Please, just sleep in the bed." I couldn't imagine how he'd get comfortable, especially with his ribs and leg still bothering him.

"I'll be fine. I was thinkin' I might try out the tub and relax in there—I think it'd feel good on all my injuries. Do you mind?"

I blinked, my stomach dropping. Wait, what? "Do I mind..."

"If I monopolize the bathroom for a while and take a bath?" He gestured toward the bathroom.

I swallowed, trying not to choke.

"Oh, yes. Of course. Or, no, not at all. Have at it. I'm all set. I'm just going to read." I patted the bed. "I'll be right here just... reading."

"Sounds good," he said, then grabbed some clothes from the closet before he entered the bathroom and disappeared from my view.

I thought maybe I'd be the weird woman fantasizing about her husband in the tub just a room away while I sat there in bed, but the exhaustion paired with the most comfortable bed I'd ever slept on, the fluffiest comforter creating the perfect cocoon... I had no chance. I never heard Noah come back into the bedroom or grab the second duvet off the bed.

I did hear a low, anguished groan around five a.m. and sat up quickly. With a glance, I saw him sitting on the side of the little reading nook area, his injured leg outstretched and his head bowed. Even from a few feet away, I could see he was tense and he'd drawn his shoulders down like they were bracing against pain.

I hopped out of bed. "Noah, what is it?"

"I'm just stiff from how I slept. It'll be fine." He didn't raise his head, just stayed there, gripping the cushion on either side of his body.

I dropped into a crouch, my body below his, and looked up at him with a hand on his leg over the soft flannel pants he'd brought to sleep in. "Do you need some medicine? Or do you want to go back to sleep? Just come lie down on the bed."

"Nah, I'll get up. I probably do need some painkillers, but I should eat somethin' since we never actually had dinner last night." He gave me a small smile, which I returned.

"Let me go see if I can grab something from that little drink area. They had a fruit basket that I bet has something, at least." I was already moving when I spoke, pulling out jeans and a shirt, hustling into the bathroom to change, and then slipping into my sneakers and grabbing a key. "I'll be back in just a minute!"

I made it down the long hallway and two flights of stairs, and across one large relaxation area to the drink station. They had little trays you could load up—*genius*. I filled a tray with water while cappuccinos sputtered into waiting mugs from the coffee machine. I found apples, plums, a banana, and a little setup that looked like it would be toppings for something. With more snooping, I discovered a lidded vat of yogurt, so I made us both bowls of yogurt with something that looked like granola but was labeled *muesli*, and shoveled a few spoonfuls of nuts into a napkin in case he'd like those.

Funny, I'd never even thought about how little I knew about his eating preferences. Hopefully, he'd be able to stomach something from this selection, and then he could take some medicine. Adrenaline and an odd primal need to take care of him and solve his problems drove me back to the room in record time.

By the time I returned ten minutes later, lightly winded from my speedy climb up the stairs carrying the heavy tray, Noah hadn't moved.

"Do you think you can move over here to the table?" I set the tray on the pristine glass surface and had a flash thought of how I could never have a table like that in my kindergarten classroom. It was a pretty obvious thought, but it sent a pang of missing my kids through me, and I made a note to check in with the sub to see how they were doing.

He pushed up and balanced against the wall, then slowly walked, watching his leg with every ginger step.

"It's already a bit better than when I woke up. It's my ribs too, though." When he sat down with a big slump into the chair, he looked at me with his big blue eyes and frowned. "Sorry, I'm a mess."

I stopped unloading the tray and sat in the chair next to him, took his hand, and pinned him with my attention. "You are not a mess. You've been through something insane. I can't even believe you're doing this well. I never should've let you drive yesterday, and I definitely shouldn't have let you sleep in that—"

"Katie, you didn't *let* me do anything. I wasn't about to ask you to drive us three hours when you've never driven in Germany. I was hardly in pain until the last little stretch anyway, and the bath last night really helped. I didn't think it'd be an issue." He squeezed my hand and let go. "Thank you for gettin' all this. It looks great."

Satisfaction at helping him surged, even if I felt frustrated he was in pain and more than a little responsible. I could do better. I would.

We each took sips of coffee, then dug into our yogurt and fruit feast. I watched him shovel bites of the granola and yogurt, gulping it down with a wince, and then drank his cappuccino like a chaser.

"Big fan of yogurt, huh?"

"No, but I know it's the best option for keepin' the meds from killin' my stomach."

Killin'. A stupid moment for that accent to get me, but it did. Then I inspected him, noticing the tightness of his jaw and the tired strain in his eyes. "Speaking of, where are they? Can I get them for you? Let's get them working so you can have some relief soon."

"They're in my dopp kit hangin' in the bathroom—outside pocket. Thank you."

That he let me do it and didn't argue, especially after getting the food, spoke of his discomfort. The frantic swirl in my belly indicated my own unease with his pain. I needed to fix it—any way I could—and fast.

I found his toiletry bag, or what he'd referred to as a "dopp kit," a little tri-fold hanging thing not unlike mine, though about a third the size. In the outside pocket, I found two pill bottles and took them both. On the way to the table, I grabbed the tall glass carafe full of water that had been sitting on one bedside table last night. I had to appreciate that they didn't use plastic bottles or expect to charge us five bucks a person just to have a sip of water before bed.

I handed him the bottles, then filled his now empty water glass. He popped two pills into his mouth, gulped down some water, and sat back with a big exhale.

I watched him, wondering what was going on in that golden head of his. He looked out the window—or where it would be once we pulled back the curtains—staring in a sort of daze. I wondered if he was remembering what he'd been through. It'd only been days since they'd found him and brought him to Germany, not yet even the same amount of time he'd been in captivity.

"You okay?"

His brow furrowed, but he looked over at me and his expression cleared. "Yeah. Meds should kick in here soon."

My heart ached for him, but I couldn't press and make him talk about what had happened. I knew better than most that a person had to be ready for that. But I could take care of his physical pain, and I would from now on. "You're sleeping in the bed tonight. I'll take the nook."

"Not a chance. That place is deceptive, and I think even if I didn't have injuries, I would've been in bad shape. If you're up to it, you sleep on one side, I'll sleep on the other. We have separate comforters anyway, and unless you sleep like a starfish, it'll be fine." He stacked his spoon and bowl back onto the tray in the middle of the table.

I'd planned to make the same suggestion myself. I'd wanted him to sleep in the bed last night, and though I would've taken the reading nook, the large bed could accommodate us both. In fact, it appeared to be two separate beds pushed together because I could see the supports for either smaller side running down the middle at the foot of the bed, though the mattress was all one. The separate duvet covers made it easy. It'd be far less intimate than sharing a blanket and needing to snuggle up with someone.

And yet... the thought of him next to me in the bed had me feeling a little dizzy.

"Katie? No pressure. I'll figure somethin' else out if—"

"No. No, it's fine. I'm sorry I spaced out. It's a huge bed, and I know you're not—I mean, I'm not worried." Heat crept into my cheeks. I didn't especially want to sit there feeling flustered, so I shuffled over to the curtains and pulled them back, revealing the rising sun and misty morning.

"Wow."

"It's amazing, isn't it?" The awe in his voice reflected my own.

"It is." I glanced at him with a smile, then opened the door and stepped out onto the balcony, breathing in the cool spring morning air. I loved the view, yes, but I needed space from him. I couldn't continue sitting there staring at him without pestering him. I wanted to know if he was okay—*really* okay. I needed to know, and yet I had no right to the information.

For the fiftieth time in the last few weeks, I felt the frustration with our situation—the forced, and yet lack of, intimacy.

So rather than continue to blush like an idiot, and at the same time grow increasingly frustrated that I couldn't hug him or hold him or beg him to tell me how he felt, I turned to the view and inhaled slowly, hoping to draw strength from the sight.

CHAPTER TEN

Noah

The pain eased after taking the meds, and finally, the breakfast meal window opened. I'd woken to pain, but also raging hunger. And honestly, I kind of hated that feeling after being its fast friend for a while there.

By the time we'd eaten our fill of the buffet, which presented a true menagerie of foods, I felt stuffed and exhausted. I'd not stopped eating until I got to that uncomfortable, too-full place, and though I didn't regret it, I didn't want to do anything that involved standing up.

"I may lie down for a nap," I said, still not sure how much to share with her. Did we need to make plans together? Did she expect that? Was it cruel of me to leave her to herself when she came here with me, didn't speak a lick of German, and would otherwise be waking up to her normal life in the US if it weren't for my royal screw up?

Or, if we believed everyone who chanted it repeatedly, not *our* screw up, but just a terrible situation that had ended well enough for us when all was said and done—thanks to the EMF guys who'd rescued us. Which I also couldn't talk about.

"Okay, that's good. You should rest as much as you want. I might go check out the pool and spa area."

She grabbed a few things from the closet and slipped into the bathroom. I lowered myself gingerly to the bed. I'd made the mistake of sort of slumping into place last night, and the impact of that idiot move had stolen my breath for more than a minute. I'd learned my lesson and from then on, I'd moved carefully.

She emerged a few minutes later, just as I was plugging in my phone and reaching for my book.

"Anything I can get you before I go?"

Eyes on her face. Eyes on her face. I repeated the phrase and did my best not to take in the full picture. Her hair was down in those loose brown waves I wanted to touch, resting just over her shoulders. The bright white robe provided by the resort was clearly made for someone shorter—it fell right at her knees rather than lower. I'd worn my men's extra-large robe last night, and it'd come to mid-calf. The long stretch of leg below the bottom of the robe and going to the ground threatened to pull my gaze, but I refused. *I refused.*

"No, I'm all good here. Just going to read until I fall asleep. I'll look forward to your review when you're back." I smiled a bland, no-big-deal smile, and she nodded, pocketing her phone and a key as she went.

At the click of the door, my head fell back against the padded headboard and I swear, I tried not to wonder. What was she wearing under there? A swimsuit? *Nothing?*

I groaned and pressed the heels of my hands into my eyes. "No, no, no. Not good."

I texted my mom, updating her on the first night, promising I'd stay ahead of the pain, and checking in on the cow that was pregnant and about to pop any day now. None of it served to remove the image of Katie in her robe from my mind.

After hanging up, I exhaled loudly, lay down fully, and tried to read my book. I had no memory of the few pages I read before I mercifully passed out.

"Noah, wake up."

My eyes shot open and my heart didn't just beat faster, it all-out sprinted. Katie's face and voice registered before I could react and do something stupid.

"I'm so sorry. I didn't mean to scare you." Her soft voice sounded genuinely upset, and she clutched her hands to her chest.

"Don't worry. You just startled me." I maneuvered my way into sitting upright on the bed. "I guess I'm still a little jumpy after—"

My words caught. Apparently, saying it out loud wasn't high on my list of things to do without thinking. Fine.

She stood there in the robe again, her hair pulled into a bun on the top of her head. Her face had a reddish tint to it, like maybe she'd been in a hot tub or sauna before she came back. Germans loved a good sauna. My XO's house had a sauna in the basement back at Kugelfels. It was insane.

She sat down on the duvet next to me. "Do you think you should see someone?"

I chuckled. "Definitely. I'm not about to pretend being

held captive and beaten and starved is a normal thing I can handle on my own. But I had a few sessions with a psychologist who deals with intense situations like that while I was at Landstuhl. Even before you got there, they'd had me meet with him twice. Then I saw him each day until we left, and I'm supposed to call and check in with him every few days we're gone as my form of accountability."

"Oh... *wow*. That seems like a lot."

I nodded in agreement. "It is, but I get it. They wanted me to have the freedom to leave, and because of our situation, they especially wanted to give us time. It's not exactly luxurious to stay at the Army lodging, nor is it comfortable to be in my barracks room. But I've just been through something very few people have, and it's unique and possibly somethin' that will have messy side effects. So far, it's just some bad dreams. But who knows, you know?"

She paled at that, and I held out a hand to stay her worry. "It's not somethin' you should be scared of, I hope you know. I feel fine. I mean, I have a lot of mixed emotions, many of which haven't even hit yet, I'm sure. But... Well, I'm okay."

She reached up, and I thought she'd touch my face, but her hand landed on my shoulder. "I wasn't scared of you, Noah. I never could be. I'm just scared *for* you. But I'm glad they figured out a way to give you some flexibility. I guess that may be part of the reason Colonel Wolfe wanted you to attend the retreat too, right?"

"Exactly. That, and it's another way for them to ferret out whether we've got a real marriage or not."

I said it to be flippant and betray my annoyance at Allen's investigation and even his suspicion of me, but the statement settled around us, heavy and dark.

"Well, that's part of what we're doing here, right? We're

getting to know each other now so when we have an audience, we'll be more comfortable with each other." She smiled and it seemed genuine enough.

"Very true."

"On that note, I'm going to go clean up. And then how about we head to lunch together?" She patted the bed and sat up.

"Sounds perfect." Though what I wanted to say was *you're perfect*, which was a little pathetic of me. But she constantly had me thinking that. Of course, I knew she wasn't *actually* perfect, but she was rolling with this crap situation so well, it blew my mind. And it made this small, hidden part of me wonder what she'd do if I pushed a little —just a little—toward this not being all a sham.

Thirty minutes later, she'd dressed in jeans and a bright white shirt, hair silky and smooth, looking effortlessly beautiful in a way that made my stomach ache. I sounded like a broken record even to myself, but damn, she was gorgeous.

"Ready?"

I pushed up from the chair, annoyed I didn't have more energy even after what amounted to a two-hour nap. "Let's do it. I feel like an old man nappin' the day away."

After making our way to the buffet area and loading our plates, we found our little booth. Tucked into an intimate corner, the location made it feel like we were the only ones in the room. The main meals were taken in the main dining room, which looked like a five-star restaurant's floor, and supposedly the dinners were that good. I regretted that we'd missed last night's dinner, but I wouldn't have survived another minute walking around.

"So how were the pool and spa?" I pinched a slice of lemon and drizzled the juice over a piece of schnitzel.

"Gorgeous. The pool is pristine and there are skylights

all above it. The lounge chairs are so comfortable, I took a twenty-minute nap in one. And the spa area was... nice, too. I'm thinking about booking a massage for Thursday." She focused down on cutting something on her plate—a large piece of melon, it looked like.

Something about that hesitation made me wonder...

"Did you use the sauna?"

She coughed, covered her mouth, and chewed her food, studiously ignoring me for a moment while she took a drink of her water.

"Um, yes." Her cheeks blazed.

I couldn't help my grin. I just couldn't. It hadn't even occurred to me to warn her. I'd assumed she'd see signs or there'd be information posted or something. Obviously not. I chuckled and her face drained of the redness in a snap.

She glared at me. "Did you know it was a nude spa?"

I cackled outright then. "I swear I didn't. I just now realized it probably was, and I didn't warn you. I just... I forgot. I don't do a lot of spa stuff, but it's pretty popular here."

Her face had turned red yet again, maybe even more deeply. "Hmm."

I reached across and set a hand on hers. "I'm sorry. I should've thought of it. I completely messed that up. I hope you were okay."

That thought paired with the warmth of her hand under mine sobered me completely. Had she been bothered?

"Oh, it was fine. I mean, as fine as walking into a sauna and finding six completely naked people in repose on the wooden benches in there and a similar scenario in one of the steam rooms can be, but yeah." She cracked a smile then.

"I'm sorry," I said, chuckling again.

She gave me a look—something a little mischievous, if I had to name it. My stomach dropped, somehow knowing whatever she said next could do me in.

"Don't be. If anything, I learned something. I need to embrace my natural state a bit more readily. Maybe I'll just have to practice."

Katie

His eyes grew large, then he frowned and dipped his head back to his plate. "Oh... yeah."

I burst out laughing, a thrill of pleasure sounding in me at his embarrassment. "You think I'm about to traipse around our hotel room naked? You've never so much as seen my bare shoulders. I'm not about to—"

"I mean, I wouldn't stop you, darlin'."

His low voice shot right through me, and so did the intent look in his eyes. The serious face, the focused gaze. He wasn't just playing along.

Oh. Okay. Got more than I bargained for with that little joke.

"I, um—"

"Wasser?" The server held a carafe up and saved me from having to respond. The servers didn't come around very often, I'd noticed—not like an American restaurant, certainly. But this was so well-timed, I wanted to thank him.

He filled the glasses with a flourish, cleared the salad bowl by Noah's plate, and left as suddenly as he had come.

"So what do you want to do this afternoon?" Noah asked, his tone completely normal.

I guess we're just going to pretend that whole sexy low voice and suggesting I walk around naked thing didn't happen. *Fine.*

"I was debating going on a bike ride," I said, pushing away the odd drop of disappointment that came with his subject change.

I should be glad for that. What could I possibly have said in response to it, anyway? *Gee, I wouldn't mind seeing you naked either?*

We chatted a few more minutes while we ate, then returned to the room. I changed clothes and found him with a book in hand, wrapped up in his robe.

"I'm going to take my turn down at the pool. Maybe see if swimming feels okay." He rested his hand at the top of his injured leg.

"Great idea. Maybe we can go together tomorrow."

"Sure. Be careful on your ride. Take your phone." With that, he held up his book in a farewell gesture and left me alone.

Though I didn't feel all that tired, the cozy bed, which the housekeeping staff had already made up, called to me. I promised myself I could take a little nap after a good bike ride. Twenty minutes later, a man so muscular he had to be a bodybuilder had helped me select a bike and helmet, and off I went. The hotel included this amenity, like all of them, so my hand-wringing about not finding pricing for bike rentals in the brochure had been entirely unnecessary.

After walking the bike down a small street and across an intersection, I pedaled awkwardly along a path that led out to the gorgeous valley at the foot of the mountains. Little paths flanked the fields, which looked like they must still be actively farmed.

After a minute or two, my bike riding skills returned. It hadn't been all that long—I rode a bike during college. I'd had to relearn then because I hadn't ridden one much in my teen years.

I expected thoughts of Noah and the morning's conversations to flood in, but as I pedaled, the crisp spring air and the view of the mountains captured my mind and I just... rode. I didn't have the usual crush of worry or sadness or regret or even longing—so many of the feelings that'd overwhelmed me in these last few weeks.

Instead, I just took it all in. The sun high in a sky spotted with clouds. The little wooden huts dotting the fields. I'd have to ask Noah what those were for. Passing fellow bikers, walkers, and a few people riding around on golf carts, though the golf course wasn't all that nearby—all of whom acknowledged me with a subtle nod. Polite, but not the outright wave or subtler finger wag Southerners in the US tended toward. Well, not people in Raleigh, so much, but those outside the city.

After an hour and a half exploring the paths flanked by bright green grasses and little yellow and pink wildflowers, with a stop to sit on the most perfect little bench facing the mountains near one of the streams that crisscrossed the landscape, I headed back to the resort. I was eager to get cleaned up and relax before the snack time meal. I didn't normally eat nearly this much, but I felt no shame whatsoever in planning to enjoy every single meal offered while we were here.

I'd never be back. I'd never have a chance to stay at a place like this, *in* a place like this, and I'd certainly never be with him.

Ah. There we go.

As I walked the bike back into the rentals entrance, the peace I'd felt out in the valley gave way to the swirling mass of confusion, anticipation, and nerves that seemed to have set up shop in my belly.

Making my way back to the room, I wished it could be simple—the feeling that I just had to get through this, or that I was glad to be here, or... just... something that wasn't so mashed up with liking Noah so much. There'd always been an attraction, and of course, that'd grown the more I saw of him. But I'd come because I cared for him in a simple way then; in a grateful, *I'd do anything for you because you did for me* kind of way. Not exactly a transaction, but it was rooted in the knowledge that I owed him. Upending my life for a few weeks to be with him after his ordeal was nothing in the scheme of things, especially when the scheme of things was a five-year-long marriage.

But I liked him more than that simple, surface-level feeling already. Just a few days of interaction and I cared about him more than ever—maybe more than I should have. But I couldn't help it. I wanted to make things better for him. I wanted to... to... I shook my head against the insane thought that pushed in, refusing to give it purchase in my already anxious mental space.

The guilt I felt at being gone this time of year nagged at me now and then, but I'd been working to quell that by reminding myself that being here had a purpose. The too good to be true feeling that accompanied being here in this setting after the insanity of his capture and recovery hung around the edges of my mind, but I had a job to do. We needed to get to know one another before we had to act married in front of the people who could end his career if they dug too deep.

I opened the door and tossed the small satchel I'd taken with a water bottle, my wallet, and keys. My mind kept circling Noah, and me, and our time together. The more time we spent around one another, the more he confirmed what I'd always suspected. He was wonderful. Pretty much everything about him was—

With a *smack*, I bodily ran into something... some*one*.

"Oh, I'm so sor—" The words died on my lips as I grabbed his upper arms. His muscular, damp arms. Small droplets slipped over his shoulders and trailed down his firm, golden, warm skin.

"Hey, no, my fault. I left my clothes out here." Noah's hands steadied me at my hips.

I opened my mouth, but no sound came out. His hands on me, my hands on him, and his chest... his bare chest. A towel was tucked in on itself low at his waist, and my brain short-circuited. Truly. With the contact, someone must've dumped a bucket of water on the motherboard of my brain or something.

I couldn't bring anything to mind except for how much I wanted to touch him somewhere other than his biceps. Though I'd done enough covert admiring of his muscular arms, so I didn't mind having a hands-on encounter. He was ridiculous. Normal human men didn't look like this, did they?

And he smelled so good—fresh, like soap. And minty like he'd just brushed his teeth. I wanted to lean closer, maybe feel the stubble at his jaw against my palm. I wanted to—

"You okay?" He dipped his head, a half smile flashing

perfect white teeth and what looked like a sense of pleasure at having caught me when he met my eye.

"I—" I croaked, then cleared my throat. "You—"

He chuckled and squeezed where he held me, then let go. Somehow, my brain sent the message to my hands to stop caressing his triceps, because, let's be honest, that's what I'd been doing. He stepped around me, probably to get those clothes he'd mentioned, and I stayed facing the bathroom, focused hard on not turning around. But sooner than I expected, he returned and slid by me, still naked but for his towel.

His back was defined, too. Did most people even have those muscles back there? Did he secretly have a job moonlighting as a fitness model or something?

"I'm sorry, but how do you look like that?" I burst out, then covered my mouth with a hand.

His cheeks brightened, and he set his clothes down on the sink. "I don't normally have this much definition. Somethin' about not eating for a week. You should've seen me in the hospital, I looked ridiculous. A week in captivity does wonders for the six-pack."

His face had sobered and so had mine. I moved to him, finally registering the darkness at his right side. It wasn't a shadow, but a bruise. His weight and water loss couldn't be solely responsible for this, but it clearly made him uncomfortable to be ogled. And who could blame him?

I stood by him as he looked in the mirror at the counter. "I'm sorry. I didn't mean to be inappropriate."

His eyes met mine in the reflection and his expression lightened—not quite to smiling, but it eased somehow. "Don't apologize. I know you didn't... Whatever. Don't feel bad. It's weird when stuff hits me."

"I can only imagine. Did the therapist talk about that at

all?" I wanted to reach out, to hug him or pull him to me and let his head rest on my shoulder—*something*.

"Yeah, he did. A lot. So it's not a surprise that it's happening, it's just harder to handle when it sneaks up on me." He placed his hands on the counter and let his head drop, leaning on his arms.

The artwork of his muscled limbs stood out in sharp relief, but the pose spoke of feeling burdened and sad, not strong. Not like it seemed he *should* be—like if there was any goodness in this world, he wouldn't be dealing with this.

But those thoughts were a slippery slope I ran from. Because there *was* goodness in this world. And if I used bad things happening to people as a sign there wasn't anything redeemable in life, I would've given up long before I ever married Noah.

And on that note, here was a man who embodied that goodness I'd wondered about for years. He exemplified it. I knew he wasn't perfect because no one was, but he'd been good to me, repeatedly, for five years. I wanted to be good to him, too.

"What can I do?" I hated the helpless feeling, but I determined then and there I'd use this time to help him if at all possible. If I was going to miss time with my students and be here, I needed to support him any way I could.

CHAPTER TWELVE

Noah

A *nything you want.*
I knew what she meant, and that wasn't it. But what I wanted most, what felt like a cosmic imperative? Her touch.

She stood close—so close—and yet hadn't touched me since the run-in. I'd be lying if I said I didn't enjoy the stunned look, how her eyes roamed over me with a predatory fascination, and the feel of her hands on my arms.

But then the *feelings* came, and not the fun kind. The kind that reminded me I looked cut from marble because I'd been starved for a week in a windowless room. If only it'd been some masterful workout program or trimming back on beer and schnitzel. Not that I didn't spend quite a bit of time working out—I did. Fairly aggressively, even, thanks to Masters' demanding regimen for the battalion. A week without food didn't magically create these muscles. But it made them stand out, even after IVs and replenishing every-thing in the hospital.

And now, she was looking at me with those soft brown eyes, her hair pulled into a low ponytail that was kind of frizzy around the hairline from her helmet. Her cheeks were still flushed from the initial encounter minutes ago, and she smelled like fresh air and sunlight.

Did I dare? I bowed my head, my thoughts racing. *Would I regret this?*

"Maybe a hug?"

I glanced up to see surprise flicker across her face before she stepped close when I turned. She wrapped her hands around my neck, her body pressed flush to mine, and she laid her head on my shoulder. I could see her face in the mirror. Her eyes were shut tight, her forehead wrinkled like she was working to infuse me with comfort.

Tenderness rolled in waves through me, and a feeling I could only describe as *heartache* struck me square in the chest.

"I'm sorry you're dealing with this. I'm so sorry it happened to begin with."

Her breath whispered across my skin, and heat, aware-ness, and desire raced to catch up with the feelings of affec-tion. I pulled back, just enough, fully aware that standing here in just a towel with her breath on my bare skin was not a great way to maintain boundaries.

I cupped her face in my hands and kissed her forehead. "Thank you."

She pressed her lips together and smiled at me—a little shy, maybe? But this had turned out to be too intense, and the bathroom too small. And I wanted her too much.

"All right, out with you. Unless you want a show."

Her eyes widened and she coughed. "Out I go."

~

Dinner proved to be the stuff of dreams. I wouldn't call myself a foodie or anything, but I loved to eat, and particularly on the heels of my last few weeks, I embraced the feast. We'd selected our appetizers, entrées, and desserts from a menu presented to us at breakfast. The meal started with appetizers, then we were invited to go serve ourselves soup and salad from the same buffet area we got breakfast and lunch. Finally came the served entrées and desserts. By dessert, I could barely manage anything else, but I ate it anyway because it all tasted so gloriously good.

"I don't think I've eaten this much... ever." Katie sat back and blinked in a daze.

"It's been a while for me, too. Too bad we missed dinner last night, but we both would've been asleep in our soup if we'd tried." I swirled the last little bit of wine in my glass.

"True. And now that we know, we won't be missing it again."

"Yes, and we have five more nights after this." I finished the wine and set it down. She'd already moved her utensils to the side of her plate and pushed her wine glass and water back. "Ready?"

I wasn't sure what made me do it. Maybe the afternoon's run-in and subsequent conversation and hug. Or maybe the laughs we'd had at the snack time meal. Or the comfortable quiet that filled the space between us while we snoozed and read in the room before dinner. But I held out a hand to her, and she took it.

I didn't let go. We walked with our hands clasped, though our fingers weren't laced together. I thought about it, though. Her hand fit mine just right, and my brain lit up with satisfaction at holding it.

"I'm not ready to go back and sleep just yet, are you?" We wandered slowly out of the dining room, then out the double doors leading to a large deck facing the mountains.

"No, let's walk a while."

Just that, and pleasure fizzed in my chest.

Maybe it made me an idiot, but the thought that she wanted to spend more time together and draw the evening out, made me happy. In fact, despite the reason for her being here, I felt happier than I had in a long time. Sure, we were in one of my favorite places in the world, staring out at mountains I loved. And I was with a woman I'd always wondered about and wanted to know, but who'd always felt off-limits to me. It shouldn't come as a shock I found the circumstances enjoyable.

"You know, I never imagined something like this existed." Her wistful tone made me turn to look at her as we walked.

"I'm sure not when you were younger, but you've seen the nice hotels in Raleigh, right? And didn't you tell me you went on a Caribbean cruise?"

She'd sent me an e-mail to that effect right after her graduation—that she'd made those plans. I'd hoped with too much energy she'd send me photos of the trip, but she hadn't. In fact, I'd never heard any more about it.

"When I wrote you that e-mail, we had, but then my friend Sarah realized the trip fell smack in the middle of hurricane season and she wussed out. Then before we could book something else, I got in a fender bender and the guy didn't have insurance, so I paid for it out of pocket. We ended up just taking a quick trip up to Asheville for a long weekend."

So many things about that were wrong. I grunted in dissatisfaction.

"What?"

"I'm tryin' to figure out where to start. First, why didn't your insurance pay for it? Second, why didn't you tell me about that? I could've helped. I thought you were on my car insurance, anyway..."

We'd come to a stop at a railing that looked down at the pool below and the mountains beyond. She turned toward me, the twilight sky hiding much of her expression.

"I am. But I thought it'd drive the premium up even though it wasn't my fault, so I just paid out of pocket and didn't claim it. It just seemed easier." She kept her eyes ahead, effectively hiding.

"That's insane. What's the point of insurance, then?"

"It was barely over a thousand dollars. I would've paid most of that anyway because of the deductible." She didn't sound at all apologetic or regretful. She clearly didn't understand why I was bothered.

"But that's money you could've spent on your trip. You just told me you went from a Caribbean cruise to a long weekend in a nearby town. That's a stupid downgrade if you didn't have to make it."

She winced at that, and I realized my mistake, cold dread slashing through my chest. I reached out and put a hand on her arm. "I'm sorry. I didn't mean it like that."

She turned to look down at the pool, which now sparkled, lit with lights all along the base of its wall in the water and around the edges themselves. "It's okay."

That small voice shredded me. *Hell.*

I stepped close and leaned my forearms on the railing, adopting the same pose she'd just taken. "I'm sorry. I don't think you're stupid, not at all. Not in *any* way. I used the wrong word, and I won't do it again."

She took a deep breath and turned her head to me. "It's

okay. Obviously, I need to work on not being so sensitive. I'm not normally. I swear I've worked through all that... baggage. Not that it's not there. I don't know why it's cropping up with you. I need to work on that."

"No. You don't. I was wrong to say it, and you're right to be bothered. I know better than to talk to you or anyone that way. What I meant to say was that I hate you didn't get to take a fancy trip to celebrate your accomplishment. You worked your butt off gettin' your degree and overcoming everything. I was happy you were doing a big thing for it. I want—"

I stopped myself there, not sure how much would be *too* much, especially on the heels of using *that* word. I'd heard her stepfather use it the day I'd met her, and from what my mom had said, it had been a common refrain with him.

"You want what?"

I turned to face her, close enough now to see her beautiful brown eyes, the long lashes that looked longer with the makeup she'd worn for dinner. The gloss on her lips glinted in the low light, and I swallowed against the rush of wanting that hit me then. My eyes searched back and forth between hers, wondering if she could hear the low thudding of my heart. If she knew how I teetered on the edge of doing something irreversible.

When I spoke, my voice came out quiet and rough. "I want you to have every good thing, Katie. Every one."

"I want that for you, too."

CHAPTER THIRTEEN

Katie

He didn't kiss me.

Of course he didn't. I shouldn't have been let down, but the disappointment had hung on me for a while —all the way back to the room, in fact. He'd said such sweet things, not just apologizing for using that awful word, but he'd meant it. I knew he had. And then he'd been so intense, focused on me.

I could've sworn he'd had the look like he wanted to kiss me. Like he was *going* to kiss me. His eyes had darkened in a way that spoke for him, and I'd held my breath in anticipation. But then another couple had come stumbling and laughing, kissing and screaming, to fall into the pool. We'd both startled and gaped before the couple broke back through the water and splashed at each other. We laughed then, the tension between us draining away, replaced by that dreaded disappointment.

He hadn't taken my hand again when we'd walked back to the room. And now I sat, staring at myself in the mirror as I took off my makeup, wondering if I could really sleep next to him.

I mean, of course I could. We wouldn't be touching in any way, but I wanted to be closer to him, and with the letdown of no kiss, I felt not only disappointment but also embarrassment. I'd confused his normal kindness—that typical Noah, amazing, over the top kindness—with interest. With meaningful attraction instead of just physical appreciation.

I could see he didn't think I was ugly or anything. I'd noticed him check me out a time or two, and the thrill that'd brought was no small thing. But I couldn't pretend he'd ever act tongue-tied or mushy-minded like I so often felt when he was close.

"You all clear? Am I okay to come in?"

He called from the bedroom since there was no door and no way of signaling we were done with our intimate business.

"Come on in," I said, lowering my face to the sink to wash.

I felt him stand next to me at the other sink, then heard him begin brushing his teeth. After drying my face, I peeked over at him but found him watching me.

He took his toothbrush out for a moment. "I like your headband."

I chuckled and pulled off the Cookie Monster headband. "Thanks."

"Sesame Street lover?" he asked, then continued his brushing.

I smiled in answer, prepared to leave my response at that. But some persistent part of me wanted him to know, to have a better picture of me. Both what he'd saved me from, and who I was now.

"I watched Sesame Street when I was little—before my mom remarried the first time and then got into drugs after he died. I always loved Cookie Monster because he got to be messy and eat cookies. I thought he was so silly, and I remember wishing so vividly I could hold his hand. I just knew it'd be warm and soft and nice."

A rush of memories assaulted me. "I still remember my mother introducing me to Jerry, my first stepfather. They'd met at a church she'd started attending when I was four, I think. He was extremely strict, and I don't remember ever having homemade cookies like I did before he came. Or being able to make messes, for that matter. No more finger painting or sidewalk chalk. No visits to the park and playing in the sandbox. I don't remember holding my mother's hand again."

I found his eyes in the mirror where they watched me, wondering how he'd respond even as I swallowed back the crush of sadness. I'd never told him about Jerry or any of that. It wasn't the worst part of my story. He knew more about Randall, the man who'd been married to my mother when he and I met.

He turned to me and took my hand, effectively skewering my ability to hold back tears. They weren't huge sobs, but a few tears escaped over my lids.

"I'm sorry, Katie. I hate that you didn't have that closeness with your mom. I hate Jerry for not lettin' you be a kid, and for gettin' your mom started on drugs. I'm guessin' that's what eventually led her to Randall?"

I sniffled and grabbed a towel to wipe my eyes. "Actually, no. Jerry died—heart attack or something. I was eight. She was sad, but we kept going to that church and they took good care of us. About two years later, we moved for some reason I never figured out. It was a super small town in Idaho, and there wasn't much there but Randall, I guess. My mom liked him enough to go out with him a few times, and not long after that, she started acting differently. I'm not positive, but I'm guessing in retrospect that's when she started using."

He squeezed my hand and brought me close, wrapping his arms around my shoulders to hug me to him. After a moment, too short if you asked me, he pulled back. "I never asked before, but I've always wondered. What brought you to Kentucky? I always thought it was pretty odd you'd just shown up."

I rolled my eyes at the memories. "We moved from Idaho to a town in Kansas, then eventually to Kentucky. I didn't realize what was happening the first time, but after the move to Kentucky, I realized we'd moved because Randall had gotten into trouble with law enforcement. He was a dealer, but I think in Kansas is where he got involved with human trafficking."

"Damn. Did he try to... hurt you?"

"No, fortunately. At that point, I was fourteen, so I suppose he could've. Not that age makes any difference to sickos, but I think he knew my mom would report him if I disappeared, no matter how high she got. I didn't think he was involved in that again in Kentucky, at least not at first. Well, not until the end when I definitely knew. I was either in my room or at school, and when I could escape, at the library. I kept my interactions with him and his nasty son to a minimum." The sneer in my voice at my stepbrother's mention was clear.

Noah's face hardened at that, too. "I always hated that

guy. I never saw him around you, but I remember seein' him harassin' Jenny Harris one day in town."

I saw the thought cross his mind before he said it, so I spared him the asking. "I left before he had a chance to do anything too bad."

"What does that mean?"

"It means he tried. He smacked me around fairly often, or he'd grab my arm really hard and leave a bruise. He groped me once and talked like he was going to do more, but I slept with a really good lock on my door from the inside. They thought they were locking me in, but most of the time, I was locking them out."

Noah's gaze had fallen to the floor, but suddenly he looked up and pulled me to him and held me there, dropping his head so his face pressed into my neck. "I wish I could take all of that away. I hate hearin' it, but more than that, I hate you had to deal with any of that. I wish—"

I pushed him away enough to see his face. "You took me away from that, Noah. You gave me a safe space. I don't know what would've happened if I'd stayed after I turned eighteen. I wish I would've been capable of getting away on my own, but I didn't know how. You gave me that and so much more."

He shook his head. "You gave yourself that. You reported them to the cops when you saw the beds, and you asked my mom for help when you knew you needed it. You did everything you could."

My eyes filled again, but I gritted my teeth against crying. Anytime I thought of the room I'd found in the storm shelter in the barn, my heart broke open. Filthy cots lining the edge of the room. Emptied water bottles and protein bar wrappers. Buckets in a corner. One set of handcuffs left. I'd run out and rushed into the house to call 9-1-1.

They'd never allowed me to have a cell phone. But the same thing that'd horrified me—that there'd been people kept in there and I hadn't known—had kept Randall and Roger from any actual jail time. They'd somehow convinced the police they didn't know the girls were there. I'd always wondered if someone with power in the town had pulled some strings.

When my mom had slurred a mention that they were coming back from jail in a month rather than the years or decades I'd assumed, I'd packed up a grocery bag of things and ran to Mrs. Miller. I was hysterical when I got there, blubbering unintelligibly. I knew if they came home and I was there, they'd kill me. They'd do it outright, and based on what'd happened, they wouldn't face charges.

I'd stayed with Mrs. Miller after that, even knowing they'd come for me there, too. But she had a plan, and thank God she did, because who knew where I'd be now.

I took Noah by the shoulders and looked into his eyes. "I will never be able to thank you for what you did for me. Never."

The muscle at his jaw flexed, and I could tell he was clenching it. His Adam's apple bobbed and he sighed.

"We're goin' to stop goin' around and around about this. I'm pretty sure I told you years ago you've got to stop that. It's not like I've gotten nothing out of this. I don't want you makin' me into some kind of hero. I *am* glad we got you out and got you safe. And I'm proud, if I'm allowed to say it like that, that you've done so much for yourself since."

I nodded once, warmth bursting in my chest. His pride in me and his insistence that I'd used the time well mattered more to me than it should've. And there was no way I could acknowledge the value his pride held for me without betraying just how much *he* mattered in many ways. So I cleared my throat and nodded again. "Okay. I'm going to bed."

I left him to finish his routine. I'd changed into a T-shirt and shorts. They were on the small side, but I'd be in the bed most of the time. He didn't seem to notice or mind, plus this was bedtime and there was a certain necessity for us to dress for bed. That was part of the awkwardness—the unknown of sharing a room with one bed. And yet, so far, I'd felt less awkward and more eager. Well and confused, a little sad, and full of memories I wished would just... get lost.

To distract myself from all the discussion in the bathroom, I tossed my clothes from the day into the little mesh bag I'd brought for dirty items and made a mental note to see about laundry services here. I'd need to do some again before we left. I'd tossed everything I could think of in the bag when I'd packed, and I'd started packing the day after they'd notified me Noah was missing.

It had kept me occupied while I waited. So I'd packed for any and every scenario. I had lots of comfortable clothes, a few nice items if I needed to go to meetings or meet people, a dress, a swimsuit... Honestly, I had one of everything, and my beast of a suitcase held it all. The bag had been overweight, but I didn't have to pay. Maybe that was because they'd booked me on a military flight.

I slipped into the bed and fluffed the comforter around me, sank back into the pillow, and sighed.

"Looks cozy." Noah's deep voice reached across the room.

I cracked one eye to see him standing in a threadbare shirt and his flannel pants. My heart rate skyrocketed at his sleepy expression and his comfortable clothes. What would it be like if he were coming to bed to sleep with me—*really?*

"It is. I think you'll feel much better sleeping on the bed."

He flashed a small smile. "Thank you for sharin' it with me."

I closed my eyes and exhaled slowly, willing myself to dream of Noah and his sweetness. To only think of his voice talking about sharing a bed and mentally banishing all thoughts of life before this moment.

CHAPTER FOURTEEN

Noah

The sound shook me from sleep. I looked around frantically but saw nothing amiss in the dim light.

Then it came again—a low, resonant sound next to me. Something like "Go," but anguished. Pained.

"Katie?"

No answer. I sat up, the room still and silent until she thrashed and it sounded like she was crying. I reached for the bedside lamp and flipped it on, then shook her shoulder. It took longer than I would've thought, but finally, her eyes popped open and she focused on me, blinking furiously through tears.

"Baby, you're havin' a dream. You're okay. You're here at the hotel with me in Germany. You're safe in this room."

Her eyes fluttered shut, and she exhaled harshly, though it sounded relieved. "Thank you."

She scrubbed her hands over her face and collected the

hair that'd crept in and crowded around her, twisting it together and then laying gently on the pillow.

"You okay?"

"Yeah."

Her voice seemed shaky and small, but it was two in the morning, so it could've just been that. I wanted to gather her to me and hold her, reassure her she'd be fine. She was safe. I would keep her safe.

After that, we lay there in silence for what felt like hours, but a check of the clock showed it had only been twenty minutes. I rested on my side—the one without bruised ribs—and watched her. I tried not to stare, of course, but it was hard not to want to keep a close eye on her. She lay on her back, staring unblinking up at the ceiling.

My gaze traced her profile—the sweep of her lashes around her brown eyes, the slope of her nose, the dip of her lips down to her chin, then her smooth, delicate neck.

Before I thought better of it, I asked, "Any chance you'd want to snuggle?"

A half-smile tugged at her mouth before she turned her head. "Snuggle?"

"Yeah."

It felt important, this moment. Probably both more and less than I realized, but it had implications for us. I didn't want to cross any lines, but the need to hold her, both for her sake and my own, gripped me to the point of desperation. Laying here watching her stare into the dark, wondering what kind of terrible memories or thoughts she battled... I needed something to do, but I needed her permission.

The thought jumped through my mind unbidden, as all such thoughts did. *If she were your real wife, you'd already be holding her.* Yeah, yeah. Thanks for the reminder.

"Okay." More than a whisper, but her voice still had that thin, shrunken quality.

I inched toward the middle of the mattress and moved my pillow, then held up my top arm in welcome. She scooted over so she was close, but not quite touching me, still on her back. She didn't know what to do, based on the way her eyes were wide and watching me.

"Turn over and get closer."

She rolled away from me, then backed up slowly until she was close enough for me to wrap my arm around her waist and pull her flush against me. We were nested together now, her back to my front, and slowly, *slowly*, I felt her relax against me.

"This okay?"

"Yeah, it's good."

Relief and pleasure swept in at that. I wanted her to feel safe with me, and I wanted that to extend to being physically close. I'd hold her the rest of the night if it'd keep her from whatever nightmares were stalking her.

In the end, that's what I did. I woke to her tucked against me, only her back moving slightly with her breath. I wished she wasn't facing away so I could see her face relaxed in sleep. My right arm and shoulder were completely numb from hours without movement. My ribs and leg ached, and I needed to move and stretch, but I wouldn't until she woke.

The closeness was getting to me. The intimacy of waking to her scent and my hand at her hip, touching her over what looked like the smallest pair of shorts in human history... *Golf. Bailing hay. Riding the combine for hours in the August heat. The shot line in basic training.* I thought of anything but her softness so close to me.

Mercifully, she moved—just barely—but enough to extricate myself from her and flee before I embarrassed us both. A few minutes later, I returned to the bedroom to find her on her back, arms stretching overhead with her back arched and—*nope*. I whipped around to bury my head in the closet.

"Sleep okay?"

"I did. Thank you."

I sifted through a stack of shirts, not really seeing them.

"Of course. No problem," I said, like I'd given her a ride somewhere or offered her a bottle of water. Not like we'd slept spooning for more than half the night.

"I'm glad."

I kept my attention pinned to the closet, hoping she'd take a turn in the bathroom or do something other than lay there looking like heaven in a bed where I slept.

"Noah?"

"Yep?"

"Can you turn around?"

I swallowed, or maybe gulped, but I convinced myself she couldn't hear it. Yes, I could turn around. That was a thing I could do. No problem.

My throat dried out at the sight of her kneeling at the edge of the bed, face expectant and pleading. I did not allow my eyes to stray from her face any more than they already had at first glimpse.

I exhaled rather loudly because seeing her like this hurt. It actually physically hurt.

"Thank you." She said it slowly, but fervently, filling the words with ten layers of emotion and significance.

"It's no big—"

She moved from the bed to stand in front of me in a flash. "Don't say it's no big deal. You woke me from a nightmare, then held me all night. *All* night. I can't imagine how uncomfortable that must've gotten, but you didn't move or wake me or anything. So thank you."

Then she did it.

She threw her arms around me and hugged me, pressing into me, all of her soft and warm. I should've felt guilty for relishing the contact like I did, but God help me, the woman was my wife and she'd slept in my arms last night for the first time. I was a mess over it.

"You don't have to thank me." I cleared my throat of the impulse to call her *baby*. I'd done it twice already—it'd just jumped out. "I want to be here for you whenever you need it."

I'd wanted to do more for her all these years. I'd always assumed I would, but she didn't let me. The car accident and insurance thing provided a perfect example. She should've told me. I could've taken care of that. I made more than enough. Plus, she lived in a studio that only used about two-thirds of what we got for housing allowance, and she insisted I take the rest. I'd been putting that away, saving all the extra we'd gotten over the years. For what, I never had decided. But I figured once we divorced, I'd figure it out.

"Well, still. I hate that dream. It's always the same. I haven't had it in years, but I'm guessing talking about everything last night brought it up again." She stepped back, my hands reluctantly releasing her, and then she searched the other side of the closet for her clothes.

"I'm sorry talkin' about it brought up the dream. But I'm glad you were able to rest after." Arms full of my clothes now, I stepped around her, avoiding taking in the perfect lines of her body as she bent and dug through a drawer. "I'm just going to hop in the shower, and then I'll be done in there. Did you want to hit breakfast?"

"Yes and yes. I'm starving."

I continued into the bathroom, focusing on going through the motions of the shower, dressing, making sure my hair didn't look like too much of a mess. I thought about shaving, but decided against it—there were only so many opportunities not to shave, and the stubble was coming in okay after forty-eight hours razor-free.

Throughout the process, I couldn't help noticing the light, happy feeling that'd replaced the mild nausea, shame, and disquiet that had built a home there since waking as the medical team wheeled us off the plane in Germany. Being with Katie made me happy and hopeful. I had so much to learn about her. There was so much more I needed to know, and for the first time ever, it seemed like I might get to.

CHAPTER FIFTEEN

Katie

We spent the next two days together.

The first two days here, we'd each done our own thing. That was partly because he'd been so sore and tired, but also because we didn't know how to be around each other constantly. We'd never spent this much time together, not by a long shot. But the night after he'd held me in the wake of my nightmare, we'd made an unspoken agreement not to leave each other's side.

This suited me just fine.

And right this moment? It suited me *just fine, indeed.*

Noah—and his gorgeous chest—was stretched out on a long wooden bench below me in a sauna. The day before, we'd wandered around the small town, stopping into little gift shops and browsing outdoor recreation stores, of which there were three. We even stopped into the grocery store and he told me all about his favorite German products and explained the way they used glass bottles and returned them to get money back. It seemed pretty smart to me.

Today, we'd taken a two-hour hike. He promised me he'd be up to more soon, but as I wasn't an avid hiker in my day-to-day life, I didn't mind keeping it short this first time. We still had two days before we'd leave this paradise and head to... wherever we'd go for the retreat.

I shook off that thought. I didn't want to think about whatever came next. I wanted to be here, now.

And especially right here and right now. Because Noah had mentioned being sore after the hike, I'd suggested a trip to the spa to use the jacuzzi, sauna, and steam room to relax. I thought maybe the heat would help his soreness, too.

We'd started with the sauna so we could get nice and hot before going for a swim in the pool. Though neither of us were comfortable enough to go naked, I'd worn my bikini, and he had his swimsuit under the towel knotted at his waist.

Or, I assumed he did. He had to. Noah wouldn't be comfortable just going for it... Or, well, I didn't think he would, but—

"I can hear you thinkin' from here."

I smiled at that. The *thinkin'* was so distinct, so him. I wondered if Germans had a harder time understanding people with Southern accents.

"I was just wondering what you've got on under that towel." I covered my mouth with my hand, surprised I'd said it aloud. Not shocked, though, because the question had consumed my mind for the last minute.

His chuckle sounded low and almost sinister. "Oh yeah?"

I stared at the ceiling of the small wooden room, the darkness lit only by a yellow light at the far corner and tiny dotted lights around the edge of the heating element. This conversation could go nowhere but toward me embarrassing myself.

"Yeah, I mean, just give me fair warning so I can avert my eyes if necessary. I might need to go dip in the pool to cool off in another minute." My skin glistened, the dry heat of the sauna warming me. Too much longer and I'd start to feel sick.

"You don't have to avert your eyes."

Something about the way he said it—all quiet and inviting. He didn't say, "*Yes, I'm wearing a swimsuit*" or "*Of course, I'm covered*" or "*You're crazy and of course you should.*" No, he said, "*You don't have to.*" Like, if I wanted to, I could look.

And now, the thing I wanted to do most in the world was roll to the side and look. Just a quick peek to see if he was teasing me. He had to be. He lay on the lowest bench right inside the door, and if someone else joined us, he'd be exposed. Granted, that didn't faze native users in a spa like this, I guessed, but I just couldn't imagine him going for it. So he had to be teasing.

Had to be.

Right?

Before I could torture myself any longer, he burst out into a laugh, filling the small space with the sound. "You're over there agonizin' about whether I'm sittin' here with my junk hangin' out for all to see, aren't you?"

I sat up on one elbow to find him smiling over at me where he sat fully upright. This brought his head about even with mine where I was propped up just a bit.

"I admit I was. Just a little. Just worrying for the poor unsuspecting person who'd come in and see." I joined in his laughter, though he'd turned silent and dropped his head.

"Seriously, it's not *that* funny."

He recovered and hit me with a look that made me warm and tingly. It was all sweet heat and kindness.

"It was pretty funny, but then your face after... That was perfection."

"I'm so glad I could amuse you."

He smiled at me, seeming genuinely pleased, but then his gaze slipped from my eyes and down the length of my body. He turned his head sharply and hopped up before clearing his throat, not looking back at me. "Ready for that swim?"

We sat sipping cappuccinos later that day. We had just enjoyed another delicious snack complete with asparagus soup, fresh bread, a small salad bar, and a dessert called *Kaiserschmarm*. It was pieces of German pancake dusted with powdered sugar, a side of homemade applesauce, and vanilla cream sauce. The doughy pancake strips were delicious, and even though I'd only planned to have a bite or two, I would've gone back for more and licked the plate clean if I could've.

I would miss the pampering of this place for sure. Gorgeous buffets full of fresh, amazing food. Coffee and wine whenever we wanted. I sighed in pleasure, happy to just be taking in the mountain's view and sitting quietly with Noah.

"What's that sigh for?"

His voice came out rumbly and tired and made me want to hug him.

He'd fallen asleep while I blow-dried my hair and did my makeup. It hadn't taken all that long, but he must've been worn out. The doctors, for both physical and mental health, had mentioned that the exhaustion for his body and his mind would linger, and we shouldn't be concerned. Lieutenant Colonel Wolfe had encouraged us to get away in order for him to have time to recuperate. But I think he meant to a peaceful place, not off sightseeing in a big city.

This suited us perfectly, I thought.

"I was thinking about how this has spoiled me for normal life. In a little over a week, I'll be back home, wandering around at the end of the school day ready for my snack time meal and cappuccino."

His big hands cupped around mine where they rested on either side of my mug. "You should be spoiled."

My eyes met his, and just like every time he said something sweet and earnest like this, my stomach dropped. My heart pulsed a little and my mouth dried out, my brain scrambling for how to respond.

"Well, so should you."

He kept his hands there, his gaze heavy. His blue eyes were so beautiful—the lighter blue rimmed with a darker circle outlining his irises so they looked more brilliant. I willed him to move them and never move. I wanted him to look away and stay right there. I needed space, and I wanted him closer.

My heart thundered and filled my ears. We sat across from each other in the carved wooden booth, a low hum of other conversations around us but unheard. It seemed like this moment meant something new, but I didn't know what for sure.

I desperately wanted to know.

He pressed his hands against mine, then released me. But before they disappeared back to his side of the booth, one came up and held my chin. "You've got a little sugar..."

He swiped his thumb over the corner of my mouth, and my stomach clenched at the contact.

"Thanks." I sounded weird—garbled and far off. Heat seeped into my cheeks, and I had to stop myself from licking the same place. Might be a bit much to lick his finger while we sat there.

"Of course." His blue eyes followed his thumb as he slowly slid it over the place again, and then over my bottom lip in a feather-light touch. Every atom in my body waited, urging him to do it again. *One more time!* He pulled away just before a server came to clear our plates.

We smiled at the server then nodded to each other, our silent signal we were ready to go. Apparently, we'd lost the moment. I wanted to scream at him—*what do you want?*

What *did* he want? We'd had more interactions than I could count lately that sent my little tail into a spin, and I didn't know how to handle it. Each time he joked with me or flirted a little. Or touched me or looked at me. Basically, anytime he was near me and the lines weren't completely clear—which was essentially all the time now—my resolve slipped.

The more I got to know Noah, the more I liked him. And certainly, the closer my little crush and years of caring about him from afar became caring about him in real life. Soon, all this *wanting*, all this care for a man who'd been my husband for coming up on five years, would need a place to go.

CHAPTER SIXTEEN

Noah

I'd lost my grip. I'd lost the ability to see the reasons we couldn't just be together. We were married, dammit! And not only were we attracted to each other, but we also genuinely liked each other, right? Maybe we weren't living together these last five years, but that time being connected created significant shared history. And we had a lot more in common than a lot of people. Didn't we?

Just looking at her made all the reasons, particularly that whole impending divorce thing, scatter.

Dangerously so. I'd had a half-dozen near-kisses. And though the look in her eyes told me she'd welcome it, I worried. We had a lot of time left before she went home, and if it didn't go well—if she didn't want that—then the retreat would be a disaster. I couldn't afford that.

We finished up a long, slow dinner—another delightful meal with even better company—and the tightness in my chest as we walked back to the room grew harder to ignore. I scrambled for an excuse not to walk into that room with her and do what I'd been wanting to for days.

"I'm going to make a call. I'll see you back in the room in a bit, okay?"

Her brow wrinkled, but she smoothed it almost immediately. "Okay. See you soon."

She kept walking in the direction of the room, in the direction I wanted to go too, and I scrubbed a hand over my face, turning the opposite way.

I found a quiet corner on one of the patios and leaned on the railing, then pressed *call.*

"Mr. Miller. Did you receive the documents?" Arnold Daily, my lawyer, asked.

"You know what, sir? I haven't been able to check my mail in a few weeks. That's why I wanted to call. I realized I should've much sooner, and I didn't want you concerned."

I should've called him the day I got back to Kugelfels. Or if not then, the first Monday after. He'd mailed the divorce papers, and I was supposed to look them over, sign and get them notarized, and send them off to Katie. It'd be a slow process, all the snail mail back and forth overseas, but I'd started the process early so no one would be rushed. I didn't want to have to Express documents internationally or Katie having to rush to get a notary or something.

But with everything that'd happened, I hadn't been to the community mailroom. We didn't get mail delivered to our doorsteps but rather had to go to check our APO—Army Post Office box. Easy enough, but I'd forgotten all about it, and had certainly forgotten about the papers waiting for me.

I'd checked my e-mail earlier in an attempt to distract myself while Katie got ready, and there it had been—a series of e-mails asking me to confirm the receipt of the documents.

"Quite all right, of course, but you are the one who mentioned a timeline. As far as I'm concerned, there's no rush, but you have your reasons. When you get them, be sure to review them before you sign. You can send them directly to your wife, or if you prefer to have an intermediary, you can send them back to me, and I will forward them on to Mrs. Miller."

His dry delivery, that *Mrs. Miller*—all of it—hit me wrong.

All the way wrong.

I hung up and paced a circle around the balcony, wishing... I didn't know. Not quite. Wishing things were different, I guessed. Wishing I didn't have to deal with divorce at all, even though it was fair to Katie. In theory, it was fair to me too. We could both get on with our lives and I could finally freaking date.

But the truth sat there in the pit of my stomach, and the more I tried to ignore it or deny it, the louder it seemed to shout in my mind: I didn't want a divorce. Not anymore. I didn't want to date anyone... except Katie. Just these few short days had shown me we got along, and we had crazy chemistry even without getting to act on it. We could actually work. Wasn't that worth something?

I raked a hand through my hair before unlocking the hotel door. I'd managed to burn an hour and hoped she'd be asleep, but I found her sitting in bed, the lamp shining a low light in an otherwise darkened room, and her e-reader in hand.

"Everything okay?"

She studied me when I walked in, and if she were at all

observant, which she'd already proven herself to be, she'd see my agitation.

"Uh, yeah. Just my lawyer."

"Oh."

"It's nothin'. Just checkin' on some documents he sent. Obviously, I missed them. I didn't check the mail when we were on post. Just felt like I needed to let him know why he hadn't heard from me." I couldn't bring myself to say what the documents were. Maybe she guessed, but I couldn't tell what she thought.

"Makes sense. Glad you got ahold of him."

Something about her quiet, cheery voice bothered me. "Yeah, me too. I'm sorry I ditched you, though. You okay?"

"'Course. Just reading." She waved her e-book in the air with a thin, close-lipped smile.

Yep. Something was off with her. Maybe because I'd disappeared after dinner with no warning after we'd spent an amazing day together. She wasn't an idiot. She had to have sensed I needed space. The question flashed in my mind—did she have any sense I'd excused myself because of my quickly unraveling self-control while being near her?

I envisioned myself going to her, tossing the e-book to the side, taking her face in my hands, and finally touching her plush lips with my own. In this vision, she'd eagerly reciprocate, pulling me down to her, both of us—

"Uh, Noah?"

I blinked away the movie playing in my mind. "Yeah? Sorry. I was zoning out, I guess. I'm going to get ready for bed."

And I'd take my time. I didn't imagine, even with the divorce papers on my mind, I could sit and make placid conversation while she sat there a little sad and small. She was so beautiful I felt winded just looking at her.

~

She couldn't have planned a more perfect way to drive me into madness over her. First, I woke to find her curled up, her back only inches from me. Her T-shirt had ridden up, exposing a span of beautiful bare skin leading to the ridiculously small shorts that covered so little of her. Before I could stop it, my mind vaulted into imagining running my hands over that expanse of skin at her lower back, following the trail of her spine, and sliding around her perfect curves to smooth along her legs.

Her legs really were long. I loved that she was tall. Honestly, I liked everything about her.

"Hey," she said, rolling onto her back, crossing her arms over her chest, and shutting her eyes.

"Hey. Did you sleep okay?" She wasn't asleep, but with her eyes closed, I could see her face, lovely and relaxed with a light red line down one side from a crease in the sheets. She must've slept hard in that same spot for a while.

Her eyes fluttered open, and the small smile landed like a punch to my heart. "I did. Sorry I'm crowding you."

I'm not sorry. I thought it, and strongly considered saying it, but where would that leave us? "Don't worry about it. I slept well, too. Maybe the key is you crowding me."

Her head popped up off the pillow at that. "Are you not sleeping?"

I made a noncommittal sound and looked around the room, but returned to her when she set a hand on my arm.

"Seriously, are you not sleeping?" Concern stitched her brows together, and that lovely mouth turned down at the corners.

"I'm sleepin'. Just kind of tossin' and turnin' more than usual, I guess. Nothin' major."

Terrible dreams weren't plaguing me or anything. I'd had a few, and they were stressful, but not nightmares. Mostly things like standing in a house that resembled the place where we were kept in Afghanistan, and I knew I needed to leave, but couldn't remember the way out. Or the one from two nights ago when I knew I was late for something but couldn't remember what. None of it was exactly nightmarish, but my brain must've been expressing stress over the situation. Maybe it could process the whole thing without my being conscious, and I could just move on. Wouldn't that be nice?

"I'm sorry. If there's anything I can do, just say the word." She squeezed my wrist and offered a smile, then slipped out of bed.

If I'd been a gentleman, I wouldn't have watched her go.

Apparently, I was just a man.

CHAPTER SEVENTEEN

Katie

Something had happened to my hesitancy.

Actually, no. I shouldn't make it sound like a great mystery. I knew exactly what had happened to it. I had trampled on it and tossed it out the window, bidding it adieu as it plummeted.

The chemistry between us drove me insane. I might not have dated much, but I could tell my husband was interested in me and I in him. And we were on a world-class fancy vacation. Why should we continue to tiptoe around each other like we didn't belong together?

Belong might've been a strong word, but I'd had the thought more than once. Spending our days together put the truth in my face: we had a lot in common. For people who were just getting to know each other, we really did. We had fun together and seemed to like a lot of the same things —dumb comedies and pizza and waking up early. We never had awkward silences anymore. At least, not when we were talking or doing something. The loaded silences came into the room when one of us needed to change or get in bed or do any of those intimate things that, as real spouses, wouldn't faze us.

Last night had been so dreamy, I'd been certain he'd kiss me when we walked home. But he'd had the phone call to make, and then when he came back, all the warmth and good feelings seemed to have fled.

But this morning, I'd awoken snuggled next to him—not quite touching, not like the night he'd held me. But close. And he hadn't moved away, despite there being plenty of room on his side of the mattress. When I crawled out of bed and made my way to the bathroom, I'd felt his eyes on me, drinking me in like a man dying of thirst. And in that moment, I'd decided.

Time to push.

I wanted him to make the first move. Desperately. I'd do it myself, but I hadn't completely banished the nasty voices in my head, and they still yelled loudly at times. Not so much in daily life, but in these extraordinary circumstances, they'd showed up more insistently than usual.

My fears of being a burden to him and holding him back were still alive and well. But now, I had new information, and we had a shared experience instead of an hour together every couple of years for legal matters. We had a budding friendship, at least. That didn't mean I could just go for it. I wished I could, but the horrible thought that it might go wrong kept me from that.

But at this point, it kept me from *only* that. Because the other part of me, the strong, smart, determined woman that ruled most of my life, knew Noah Miller was interested.

I'd realized that Noah was such a good man, he

wouldn't want to pressure me. He wouldn't want to seem like he was taking advantage, or whatever other nonsense might occur to him. And I appreciated that about him, particularly because I'd lived with two men who took advantage in every possible scenario and in every possible way.

But Noah couldn't take advantage of me because I wanted him to kiss me and touch me and open up more and more and let me in. I wanted him to know me like no one else did, and I'd never, *ever* had that feeling. Well, I'd never had it for anyone but him.

Confusing didn't even begin to describe it since I still had a life to get back to. None of this could last beyond what we'd already planned—the five-year mark was coming, whether we kissed or not. But that didn't mean my heart and body were paying attention to the logic that reality should provide.

I moved through the routine of blowing out my hair and doing my makeup, dumping my hesitation, and deciding I'd show him. I wouldn't be the one to kiss him, but I could flirt, and I could make his ability to resist making a move stretch thin.

Atop the Zugspitze, the highest mountain in Germany, I inhaled crisp mountain air while looking out on the neighboring peaks and the valley below. I couldn't quite see the resort from this angle, but it wasn't far.

"Ready?" Noah spoke close into my ear.

I jumped, startled to find him so close, though the surprisingly loud observation deck must've masked his approach. I'd also noticed he didn't like to be overheard talking. He'd mentioned something about never wanting to be one of those horrible, noisy Americans because he'd seen it too many times. I couldn't imagine him being obnoxious like that, but his desire not to disturb the other people around him while they enjoyed the glory of the view was just one more example of his considerate nature.

"Sure. What's next?" With one last glance out at the scene, I turned and followed him. His hand swung by his side, and my heart thudded as I considered reaching for it, but I couldn't imagine what I'd say if I did it.

So far, my big decision to push him hadn't amounted to much. There just hadn't been time to do anything out of the ordinary. We'd had breakfast, then he'd talked with the front desk about our plans for the day while I wandered the hotel gift shop, and then we had driven to the base of the mountain where we'd caught a cable car to the top. Our time hadn't exactly been rife with compelling moments, and we'd essentially had zero privacy.

"We're going sledding." He flashed his eyebrows at me, holding open the door to the inside of the covered walkway that led into the building.

"Really?"

He nodded with a grin. "There's a glacier we can get to if we take another cable car. You can sled year-round and obviously ski, too. I figured we better sled so we can say we've been sledding on a glacier in May."

"I've never been sledding," I said, following him through the turnstile to load into another, much smaller cable car.

"Really? You didn't in Idaho?" He grabbed a little loop that hung from the ceiling above to steady himself as the car rumbled along its track.

"If I did, I don't remember it. My mom worked all the

time. I played in the snow, but we lived in a depressingly flat neighborhood. Plus, once Jerry joined the picture, we didn't do much of anything except go to church on weekends." *What a jerk, that Jerry.*

"That's terrible. I'm glad we're going to rectify this."

His attention shifted out the window, so I wondered aloud. "How did you go sledding? I don't remember it snowing that often in Kentucky."

He turned back to me. "Oh, it did sometimes. But I have relatives out in Utah. We'd go out there every few years at Christmas to ski or whatever. They lived in this tiny little ski town that had a great mountain for skiing, but it wasn't pricey and overcrowded like the bigger names. It was great." He frowned, his eyes flickering around the car. "Come to think of it, I think my mom told me not long ago that my cousin had moved back there a few years ago. She'd been in New York at culinary school or something. She left the small-town life behind her and all that, but I guess she had a change of heart."

"That's pretty different from a New York City life, from the sounds of it." I couldn't imagine living in a city like that. Raleigh was enough of a metropolitan feel for me. I didn't ever want to be out in the country again. I could live my entire life without seeing another farm and be just fine. But I didn't want to live in a concrete jungle, either. I liked green. Something about it made me feel hopeful.

But this—the white that spread out in dips and hollows below us as we neared the station at the end of the line—felt like a kind of demanding beauty. And how crazy to be looking at snow in mid-May, but here we were. Even the air in the cable car had cooled as we approached the unloading point.

The car slowed and swung as it slowly entered the

station. I held tight to the hand strap above me, but I still stumbled into Noah. His hand steadied me at my waist, and even through three layers of clothing, his touch sent my pulse flying.

"Sorry." I grimaced, registering I'd stomped on his foot.

"No problem. These boots can handle being trampled on. Oh." His face sank as he looked down at our feet. "I just realized you only have sneakers. Your feet are going to get soaked in the snow."

Shoot, I hadn't thought of that either. "It'll be fine. I can hack it."

He narrowed his eyes, then his arm flexed in a move that brought me closer to him. "We'll figure something out."

The air vanished from my lungs at his closeness, and my mind did the same thing it'd done every other time he'd gotten even remotely close. *Now? Will he finally kiss me now?*

CHAPTER EIGHTEEN

Noah

Was it condescending to find someone adorable when they were mad?

Because Katie was adorable. I mean, it was irritating as all get out that she wouldn't just give in, but cute all the same. Of course, based on the glare, the arms crossed over her chest, and the frustrated harrumph she'd just let out, she probably didn't see me in a similar light.

I stepped closer to her, glad we'd moved out of the small building onto the plaza so we could talk without an audience for our little disagreement. "Just hear me out, okay? If you let me carry you, your feet won't be wet. Even if we leave here and go straight back to the hotel, your feet will be wet and freezin' cold for at least an hour. That's super uncomfortable. Not to mention, it may be dangerous depending on how cold they get."

Nothing on her body moved but her eyes, which flicked up toward me. "You're not carrying me."

"Why not?"

"Because."

I fought the urge to sigh dramatically or roll my eyes. Damn, but she was stubborn. "Why not?"

"*Because.*"

I appealed to the heavens, then stepped closer. "I'm not tryin' to be some alpha jerk or somethin'. I just want us to go have fun. Can we do that?"

Her brow pinched, and she pressed her lips together, but the tension in her shoulders seemed to lessen a little. "I am not a small woman, and you're going to be walking on snow. That's not exactly a brilliant setup. But maybe I need to spell this out for you. You. Are. Not. Carrying. Me. You're still healing, Noah. There's no chance."

I studied her face, the light slowly dawning. Of all the things I would've guessed, I hadn't thought of this one. "You're worried about me hurtin' myself. That's why?"

She huffed. "Of course I'm worried about you hurting yourself! How could I not be? I'm glad you're feeling better, but carrying me around a glacier? Not happening."

Something in my chest warmed and spread, and I reached for her. I had to touch her, to bring her close and have her near me after that show of care and concern. I wanted to pull her to me and kiss her—good Lord, did I want that—but I settled for squeezing her at the waist over her sweater and jacket. "You're pretty stubborn, you know that?"

Her lashes fluttered and the look she gave me was of pure, unimpressed annoyance, except for the tiny smile tugging at the corners of her mouth.

I exhaled, shoving away the now ever-present desire to

crush my mouth to hers. "All right then, let's go. And when your toes freeze off, I'll nurse you back to health. I'll be real gentle, and I'll only say *I told you so* once or twice."

She laughed at that and swatted at my shoulder as we walked. I offered my arm for her to hold, which she took when we hit the snow. She had on sturdy running shoes, but they'd be wet soon. The snow was fairly packed from foot traffic along the path we followed, thanks to the signs. She slipped around at first but soon figured out how to walk without sliding, maybe because the snow had some give to it so her feet sank in. They were going to be soaked inside ten minutes.

The sun shone on the snow, and the day felt like a perfect bluebird ski day. I'd enjoyed a few of those at Silver Ridge Lodge in my childhood. It'd been years since I'd been back for a visit. I had the strangest pang of longing for that time in my life—when everything was simple, and all I had to do was have fun and be nice.

I shook off that odd nostalgia when we arrived at the sledding hill—a long and decently steep slope that happily appeared to belong to us alone.

"Ready?" Katie released my arm and grabbed a sled from the pile.

"Let's do this. Ladies first, if you want."

Her grin was pure joy and hit me right in my stupid bruised ribs. She looked so happy and free, little wisps of hair fluttering around her face, the rest pulled back in a low ponytail. I couldn't see her eyes since she, like me, wore sunglasses. We would've been blinded by the glare and the bright snow had we not, so at least in that way, we were prepared. I felt so dumb for not thinking of her shoes since I'd planned this, but hopefully, it'd be worth it.

She hopped on the toboggan-style sled, then with one

last glance and giant smile back at me, pushed off. There was no sound but the whoosh and squeak of the sled on snow. And then she came to a stop, hopped off, and held her hands aloft in victory. She was far enough away, I couldn't see much but her smile.

I hopped on my sled and joined her, quickly praying I wouldn't crash and destroy myself even further. The cold air rushed into my face and my stomach dropped as I flew down the hill. I made it about twenty feet farther than her and felt the unease lighten at having made it down the slope without wrecking.

We each took two more turns separately. By the third time up the hill, I could tell I needed some rest. It was pathetic and aggravating, but I couldn't ignore the twinge in my ribs or my leg anymore.

"Want to go together?" I asked, nearing where she stood at the top of the hill, breathing a little hard from the slow trudge back up the snow.

She eyed me, surveying my entire body. I stood up straight, giving equal weight to both legs. She'd been monitoring me, I could tell, but I'd done a decent job of hiding the pain that'd started growing stronger.

"If we crash, I'll hurt you. I'm not sure it's smart." She brushed some snow off her jeans, avoiding my eyes.

She was too sweet, worrying about that. The concern should've grated on me, but instead, it made me feel mushy, fussed over. It made me feel like she genuinely cared about me, about how I felt and how my recovery went. And that made it even harder than it had been to keep from grabbing her and showing her how I cared for her.

"I'll be sure to fall on you and not let you fall on me. If I go behind you, it's more likely for that to happen anyway, right?" I grabbed a two-person sled and set it down, climbed in the back while suppressing a groan, and anchored it with the heels of my boots in the snow. "Come on. This'll be my last round."

Instead of speaking, she climbed in and settled between my legs. I swallowed, the nearness exciting. It was ridiculous considering we'd spooned in bed days ago, but even this closeness felt significant. My arms reached around her, and just that kept my pulse beating fast. The position was a thing a man would do with his woman—a sign of care, belonging.

She turned her head to look back at me, and though she couldn't turn all the way, I leaned to the side so I could see her. I couldn't see her eyes, the sunglasses still blocking them, but I could tell she meant business.

"Promise you'll fall on me."

I chuckled. Like there was a chance in hell I'd put all my weight on her. "I promise."

We both pulled our feet in, her legs resting against mine just another form of contact to keep my heart pounding. We swooped down the hill, gathering speed. Before I realized what had happened, we caught an edge or hit a rock—something. And sure enough, the sled toppled. Seconds later, we tumbled, side by side, into the snow.

I stayed still a moment, blinking into the blue sky, my sunglasses crooked on my face. I wiggled my limbs, then sat up when everything felt okay. She lay right next to me, eyes still fluttering, and concern shot through me.

"Katie, are you okay?" I knelt by her side, and she lifted her head like she might move to sit up, but then dropped it back.

"I'm okay," she said, though her voice came out strained.

"Stay still a minute." I set a hand on her shoulder to keep her from trying to get up again. My mind raced through the things to check. A neck injury would be the most dangerous. Plus, my phone might not work up here. I'd have to run back to the building and—

"I really am okay. It just knocked the wind out of me." She sounded better already, though still winded.

Relief washed over me and I exhaled loudly. "Thank God."

"Were you that worried?" she asked, now slowly sitting up and pushing her sunglasses to the top of her head.

"I might've been catastrophizin' a bit." I forced a laugh, but the adrenaline from the ride, and then the fear, still coursed through me.

She set a gloved hand on my arm and smiled reassuringly. "I'm fine."

Whether it was the relief and the small touch, or that little smile, or the look in her brown eyes I could finally see... Whether it was one or all of those things that did it, I couldn't have said. But something made me lean down, and with a gloved hand at the back of her head, bring her mouth to mine. I pressed against her chilled lips, and she tilted her face up to mine. I pulled back and released her to find her watching me, a stunned but not displeased look on her face.

At least, I hoped there wasn't displeasure. I only wanted to give her pleasure, joy, and happiness. If my touching her caused anything but that, I'd never do it again. It might nearly kill me, but I wouldn't, even if all I wanted to do was take her mouth again and lay her down in the snow and stay there a while.

I made a point of looking away, down at my watch to give me something to do besides attempt to read her expression or wait for her to say something—anything. "We should probably get goin'. The lifts close in an hour, and I think we should have some hot chocolate before we leave."

We stood and tromped our way up the hill. Her silence felt deafening, but I chose not to dwell on that. Maybe she wasn't upset, but she was thinking. I'd just changed the dynamic of our relationship. I'd succumbed to the chemistry and charge that hung around us anytime we were close. *All the time.* Of course, she had to think, to evaluate how she felt.

And hopefully soon, she'd show me.

CHAPTER NINETEEN

Katie

I didn't say much on the way back up to the lodge, or when we sat and enjoyed *heiße schokolade* on the plaza. Just a few *thank yous* and maybe another question or something. Honestly, I had no real sense of time passing. We ascended back to the structure at the top of the Zugspitze, then waited a few minutes for the larger cable car to make our descent.

All the while, I just kept thinking *finally*. Finally, he kissed me! And yet, it had been so vastly different from the kisses I'd had in my teens—all before I married Noah, and all with boys I hardly knew and certainly never cared about. Both other experiences had been rushed and mildly terrifying because I'd feared someone would tell my stepfather, or Roger would see me or hear about it, and use it for leverage against me.

Noah's kiss embodied tenderness, care, and yet a strain

of passion that left me more breathless than getting the wind knocked out of me. It'd practically broken my brain. I hadn't even closed my eyes. I'd wanted him to do that for days now, but once he had, I'd hardly reacted. At least I'd tilted my head. I hoped he understood that was all I could do. I didn't have the wherewithal to reach up and grab him, hold him to me, anything. I just... got kissed.

We hadn't acknowledged it, but I'd noticed him watching me, a slight frown pulling at his mouth. I wanted to kiss that away. But he'd been so concerned when we'd tumbled off the sled. Maybe the kiss had been one of relief, a kind of comfort measure. Maybe he kept looking at me because he worried I'd truly hurt myself and just wasn't saying.

Confusion clouded my mind. I'd been so confident this morning. So arrogant and certain I could tempt him to give in and kiss me. Of course, I'd done nothing, any chance I might've had squandered by my nerves. How had I thought I could do anything other than sit back and wait?

By the time we reached the resort, left the car for the valet, and trudged back to the room, I'd said less than fifty words to Noah. I felt terrible about it. But every ounce of shyness I'd ever owned had descended on me, ganging up on the desire to be bold and kiss him or even just acknowledge what had happened.

Something buried in me knew the kiss meant something. Something huge. And a warring element reminded part of me that a connection beyond here and now didn't make sense for us. It never had. That's why we'd kept our distance—or one reason we had. But now...

He'd attempted conversation in the car only once, asking about my shoes. They were wet and cold, but we were almost home, so I could change them. No big deal. I'd said they were fine. I cringed, walking and wishing I had learned how to flirt or interact with a man I liked at some point in life. I hadn't, clearly, and I'd never felt that more starkly than now.

We pushed into the room, and I toed off my shoes.

"I'm going to hop in the shower," I said, walking straight to the closet to get dry clothes, then disappearing into the bathroom as he said, "Okay."

What a coward. Completely. But after a hot shower that left me overheated and dressing in dry jeans and a T-shirt, I emerged to find Noah sitting on the side of the bed. He rose to his feet the second I stepped into the bedroom.

"Can we talk?"

His blue eyes were striking in the dim room. The sun must've hidden behind a cloud, and the late afternoon sky provided little natural light. He hadn't turned on any lamps, which cast a depressing dullness into the space.

He still wore the dark gray pants and green T-shirt with a long-sleeved layer underneath from earlier. I wondered if he wanted to shower before changing. Something about the combo of the utility pants and the two shirts made me crazy. Maybe it was the way it all fit him so perfectly, highlighting the curves of his biceps and the lines and dips of his torso. A torso I'd seen and admired and very much wanted to experience again.

My heart pounded. I shoved my dirty clothes into the laundry bag. "Of course. What about?"

I faced the closet, trying to find an excuse not to turn around and look him in the eye while he explained his mistake in kissing me, or whatever was coming. The feeling in the room, his demeanor... it didn't bode well, and I didn't want to deal with it. I'd worked through my impulse to hide from bad things—one ingrained in me growing up—but it roared back to life in this moment.

"Katie." His voice edged on impatient, but it wasn't loud.

I let out a large breath, steeling myself, then faced him. He'd moved closer—much closer—and stood inches from me.

He searched my face, then lifted his hand but let it drop again. My pulse raced and raced until I felt dizzy just standing there.

"I'm sorry. I didn't mean to cross a line back there. I—I didn't mean to upset you." He stepped back.

"What do you mean?"

He apologized, but he didn't say it was a mistake. He didn't say he didn't mean it. He thought he'd upset me. And of course he would; I'd been acting like I was upset. How could he possibly know my reaction was anything but upset?

He shifted from foot to foot before looking back at me. "We've never had that kind of relationship. And if you don't want that, that's perfectly okay. I don't want you to feel like I've messed everything up. I don't—"

"Noah, if you think I'm upset because you kissed me, I'm definitely not." My cheeks were absolutely on fire, which didn't really make sense because he'd brought it up. I'd never been this bold with a man, and more importantly, with him. "I'm glad you kissed me. I've been waiting for it."

His lashes fluttered, and he stepped closer, just like I did. "Then why..."

I shrugged. "I don't know what I'm doing. I don't know about any of this, and I don't want to mess anything up."

And I don't see how this can work. I didn't share the thought—didn't want *that* in the air between us.

His face brightened, and his eyes flickered back and forth between my own. "How could you mess anything up? You're amazing."

My stomach did the fluttering now as he inched closer, and I tried to nail down words to speak.

"I—I don't know. I just..." I could hardly breathe again, reaching for him. With hands on his broad shoulders, I stepped flush against him. "I really want you to do it again."

In seconds—no, less than a second—his hands held my face, and he leaned in to banish the space between us. My eyes closed this time, and the sensation of his lips on mine filled me with urgency and joy and a frantic feeling that had me gripping his shoulders, then sliding my hands up and around his neck.

His hands stayed where they'd started, cradling my face while tilting my head and deepening the kiss. A sound of approval resounded in his chest when I opened for him, and the sensations heightened, my insides turning to liquid heat. Lips and tongues and so much desire I knew if I let go of him, or if he wasn't holding onto me, I'd sink to the floor.

He pulled back, just barely, and my eyes blinked open to find him studying me. His hands still cradled my face and pushed into my hair a little. He shook his head like he didn't believe I was standing there in front of him, the barest smile on those lips I wanted back on mine.

"Why'd you stop?" I asked, breathless but still wanting his kiss, the closeness, everything.

A smile flashed, a deadly weapon at this close range. "I figured maybe we should take it slow. We may have been married for years now, but it's not like we have to dive in over our heads the same day we share our first kiss."

I unlocked my hands from behind his head and stepped back. "That's true."

He chuckled.

"Don't sound dejected. I promise you I don't *want* to stop. I'd love nothin' more than to—" He cleared his throat, looked down at his feet before back at me. "Well, the point is, we've got time, right?"

The small, almost shy smile on his face made me feel melty and so happy I couldn't help but let out a laugh. I pushed away the nagging response to his question, though. Because the answer was ugly and awful, and I didn't want to acknowledge it.

Despite his claim we had time, he was wrong.

We'd already had time, and now, we basically had none.

CHAPTER TWENTY

Noah

It didn't take as much strength as I would've expected to step away from her and take my turn in the shower.

It took a herculean amount, yes. It hadn't been impossible like I'd feared it would be. But I did. Because she'd kissed me back with enthusiasm, and though that had shot adrenaline directly into my heart, it had also calmed me. We could enjoy that part of our relationship and continue to get to know each other. We could hold hands and when I had the thought that I wanted to kiss her, I would.

Not every time. She might get sick of me. But yeah, she was open to the prospect of more physical interaction, and who was I to deprive the woman?

I didn't like the train of thought I had then—wondering how many other men she'd kissed in the last few years. I scrubbed the shampoo through my hair, trying to wash away the thoughts of her with anyone but me. I had no right to be jealous, but I was. I would've been before if she'd ever mentioned someone, but she'd been careful not to, I supposed, since she'd never said a thing about anyone else.

I shook all of that off, all of it. Kissing her twice and then storming out and demanding her dating history wouldn't work in my favor. Not that I felt I needed to tiptoe around, but I wanted us to continue enjoying the time here. We only had another full day before we transitioned to being around other people. I wanted us comfortable with each other, and to get there, we needed to just... keep talking. Keep kissing, if I said so myself. Keep enjoying each other.

By the time we'd both cleaned up and relaxed for a bit, dinnertime had arrived. Sadly, we'd missed the afternoon snack time, and already, my body had become accustomed to its regular feedings and truly felt the loss. I bordered on ravenous by the time we'd planned to leave for dinner, but when she stepped out of the bathroom in a dress, her hair loose and wavy, all thoughts of food evaporated.

"You look gorgeous, Katie." I took her hand and drew her close, then leaned down to kiss her cheek. She turned her head into the kiss, just slightly, and something about that small move made desire curl low in my gut.

"You look nice too," she said, a small smile on the mouth I wanted to taste again. Then she planted a hand on one shoulder, held my face with the other, and kissed my cheek.

When she pulled back, she smiled brighter and my stomach dropped.

"Sorry." Her voice came out just above a whisper, the sound close and intimate. Then she dove into the little purse she carried and brought out a tissue, wiped my cheek with it, and tossed it in a small trash can. "Lipstick mark."

I nodded, feeling foolish and overwhelmed. Whatever

had happened to me in the last few minutes, I needed to get a grip. I couldn't wander around like she had me under a spell, but that's what it felt like—like Katie had emerged from the bathroom in this light blue dress and put a spell on me.

"Ready?" She tilted her head, obviously finding my silence unusual, but mercifully not commenting.

I blinked back at her, then offered an arm in answer.

Fortunately, on the walk to the dining room, I recovered my faculties of thought and speech. By the time we took our seats, I'd managed to start and hold a decent conversation, and all had returned to normal. If I occasionally had to keep my eyes from tracing the neckline that dipped not quite low enough at her chest, or caught myself fisting my napkin in my lap to avoid reaching over and crushing my mouth to hers? Well, I'd say I kept my baser instincts pretty well in line.

The conversation helped. She told me about her friend Sarah and about her fellow teachers. She told me about a few kids in her class and her oddball principal.

"What is your favorite part about teaching?" I asked, leaning away from the table, my entrée plate completely empty.

Katie finished chewing a bite and wiped her mouth— another part of her I'd tried not to stare at through the evening. I had plans to spend quality time with it later. I didn't need to stare.

"The kids are the best part. That sounds so generic but they really are. Five and six are the best ages, especially by this point in the year. They've all gotten the hang of the routines, they know what's expected, and they're mostly past the big tears over things that happen." A wistful, maybe even sad smile graced her face as she swirled the last sip of wine in her glass.

"I'm sorry you're missin' this time with them." Not for the first time, I realized what a sacrifice she'd made in coming here.

She took a moment before answering. "You don't need to keep apologizing, Noah. I promise you I'm not sorry I'm here. I miss the kids, but I'll be back with a few weeks to spare. In the end, it's going to be less than three full weeks I'm gone."

She extended her hand across the table, palm up. I eagerly took it, resting mine in hers. At some point, she'd painted her nails a light blue to match the dress. She wore a simple gold band on her ring finger.

I should get her something better. How had I never done that? In the beginning, my mom had bought us two gold bands to get us started, but I should've replaced them.

It's too late now.

I flinched away from that thought and held her hand more tightly.

"What's going on in that head?" She squeezed my hand to prompt an answer.

"I was thinkin' I should've bought you a nicer ring." I pulled out of her grasp and fiddled with the simple band, keeping my focus there.

"I like this one just fine. Doesn't get in my way but still sends the message." She watched our hands when she spoke.

"What message is that?"

Her eyes found mine. "That I'm taken."

~

Holding her hand during our usual evening stroll around the resort lit up my awareness. Every now and then, our arms would brush, and the contact left tingles cascading over my skin. These simple touches combined with the conversation, her warmth and loveliness—even the stupid stars twinkling overhead—had left me nearly gasping for air around the knot of want expanding in me.

The reality that had been fast barreling toward me and had now accelerated was this: I didn't just want Katie physically. That'd never been an issue. She'd always been beautiful, but now? Now I knew how caring, how thoughtful, how funny, and how kind she was. They were all things I'd imagined from time to time, but to feel all of that directed at me was so completely opposite from what life had been like for so long.

I liked my life in the Army, but I wouldn't pretend it hadn't been lonely. And I would be a liar if I said I'd never regretted being married to someone so far out of reach. The first year or so, it hadn't bothered me. I'd been deployed, then moving, and coming out of seeing her so wrecked when we ran away and she began cobbling together a life apart from the abusive assholes who comprised her family.

But later? Yeah, I'd had some regrets. I'd wondered at whether I'd done the wrong thing by insisting we reach for year five. Why not year three? What difference did that make? Except any time it occurred to me to bring it up, I'd remember I was the sum total of her support system. If we divorced, she wouldn't have my benefits or even a military discount on tuition.

And not that I postured myself as some selfish paragon of sacrifice, because I also reaped the benefits—I made money, too. She'd always lived in a tiny studio apartment, and as soon as she graduated, she'd insisted on helping with rent. So I'd pocketed the cash difference, some months more than others, and I'd made a sizeable little nest egg for myself.

I exhaled a great gust while we walked, taking in the sight of the shadowy mountains crouching like giants in the night-darkened vista. Having her here now, I certainly felt no regret except for a sharp sense that I'd missed out. What would've happened if it hadn't been a marriage in name only? Where would we be?

"You okay?" She slowed to a stop near a little sitting area with a huge, wicker couch-like piece of furniture topped by cushions and pillows.

"Want to sit?" I nodded to the spot.

"Sure," she said, then pulled me down with her. "What's going on in that head? You're very quiet."

I brought our joined hands up and kissed the back of hers, then set it down and relaxed into the cushions of the couch. She did the same so we lay almost fully reclined, staring up at the night sky. We were completely alone out here, or at least it felt like it. Most other people congregated at one of the bars or on the patios where there was more light.

"I'm not thinkin' much of value. Just runnin' around in my head, I guess." *Just thinking about our marriage, and what would've happened if we'd done it differently.*

She rolled to her side and propped her head in her hand. "Anything you want to share?"

I smiled. She wanted to know but wouldn't push. Frustration slithered through me at the reality that I didn't know whether she just didn't tend to push, or if she felt she didn't know me enough to have the right.

"It's not much in the way of coherent thought—just little *what-ifs* and such. Nothin' too significant to give to you or that I'm keepin' to myself." I turned to the side and watched her, the little V between her brows deepening with concern. Her hair spread out behind her, over a shoulder, everywhere, alluring little glints from ambient light shining in it.

I shook my head, my stomach tying itself in a knot. It was flat-out back-bending on itself just from looking at her—just from the longing for closeness of every kind with her.

"What's that look for?" She nodded her chin to me, eyes steady on mine.

I swallowed and reached out to take a lock of hair between my fingers. "Right now? I'm thinkin' how even in the darkness, you draw me in like a star."

She huffed and looked around at the stars. "You shouldn't say stuff like that."

"Why not?" With two fingers, I turned her chin toward me until her eyes followed, the look in them once her gaze met mine so serious—so *full*—my throat dried out and my heart drummed at a sprint.

One of her hands found my shirt and gripped it at my chest. "If you keep it up, I might get confused and think all this is real."

CHAPTER TWENTY-ONE

Katie

My heart hammered in my chest as he moved closer, though there wasn't much room to go since we lay facing each other, talking in quiet voices no one walking by would understand.

"It feels real to me," he said, his words nearly a whisper.

Could he mean that? Could he be having all the same winding, maddening thoughts I was?

"Me too."

I pulled where I gripped his shirt and he moved, one hand in my hair and one at my waist. In a moment, we were connected, kissing like we'd been doing it for years. Well, I doubted that kissing the same person for five years would absolutely melt me and drive me insane. Though maybe it would if it was Noah. I pushed against him as he pulled me close, friction and heat and a kind of delirious pleasure clouding the ability to think about anything or anyone but him.

"Noah," I sighed, pulling back, my eyes fluttering open to find him resting his forehead against mine, both of us breathing heavily.

"I won't ever tire of kissin' you." His voice came out rough and delicious.

Kissin' you. Sigh. "Works for me."

He flashed a smile, then pecked my cheek and stood. "We better go. Feels like we're alone out here, but I hate the idea of being interrupted."

I took the hand he held out and rose, straightening my dress, but my heart didn't slow. Did he think we'd continue once we got to the room? Did I want to?

Yes.

I filtered through all possible feelings at the thought. Was there something wrong with being together? I'd always assumed I'd be with someone I loved, and I did love Noah. I was fast falling in love with him, too. On top of that, we were married. It didn't really get any more official than that.

But we'd shared our first kiss hours ago. It was too much too soon, and I knew it. I didn't move at this pace in any facet of my life. Well, except for when I ran away from home, married a guy I barely knew, and made a new life while hiding from my vengeful, terrifying family.

And then, of course, the fact that we planned to part in months—less than months. We didn't plan to stay together, but we *were* together. We had been for years. And we were here, now.

My stomach flipped when he grabbed my hand. Since the lounge area where we'd been snuggled was relatively close to the room, we made it back and inside in what felt like seconds. Noah led me through the doorway, shut the door, and backed me up against it.

"You got quiet," he said, planting warm kisses at my ear and down the line of my neck.

"I did."

His head popped up at the sound of my voice, and he placed a warm, rough hand at my cheek. "What's wrong?"

My stomach tumbled at his look, the texture in his voice, and those blue eyes studying me. But not telling him wasn't an option. "I'm... nervous."

A smile flashed again, and I realized his smile was a weapon against my will. He deployed them stealthily, leaving me off-balance at the sight, so whatever came next found its mark even easier.

"Aw, baby, I wouldn't rush you. I want to kiss you and be close to you, but there's no pressure here. Truly." His brows rose like he'd asked a question.

I swallowed hard against that *baby* because I liked him calling me that. And I did trust him. I had no reason to doubt him. "Okay."

He smiled again, this time a sweet, close-lipped smile, then placed a kiss to my forehead. He stepped away and offered a hand, which I took. We walked all the way into the room together, and he sank to the bed. I took a seat next to him.

He started to say something, then stopped himself. Instead, inspecting our hands clasped together between us on the bed.

"What?" I asked, anxiety building and pushing into my mind. Fleetingly, I heard that voice. *This is all your fault. You ruined the moment.*

But as he stroked my hand with his thumb, the voice receded, and the only thing left was Noah. I could've sighed in relief because the usual hounding criticisms hadn't been plaguing me—not since we'd left the hospital. I didn't know why that was, but he was clearly a key ingredient.

"We're just gettin' to know each other and trust each other, so I don't have a way of promising you I won't hurt you or that my motives are pure." He chuckled at that. "Well, maybe *pure* is the wrong word, but you know what I mean?"

"I do trust you, though. I don't want to seem... reluctant to be with you. I want to, I just... Today..." My gaze broke from his because he was too handsome sitting there next to me in his collared shirt, that gorgeous face, and his hair just a little askew. His eyes were so earnest and intense.

"I get it. I agree. After nearly five years, we're not about to go from our first kiss to sleepin' together in one night. Well, *sleeping*, yes." He nudged me with his shoulder and wiggled his eyebrows, then we both laughed.

Some of the tension that'd built since his comment outside seeped out, and a wave of appreciation flooded in at his ability to calm that storm in me and relax us both.

"I'm sorry. I don't mean to get uptight. I care about you and I want to..." I faded out and he turned to me.

"Please, don't apologize for talkin' to me. Or for feelin' how you feel, however that may be. I am nothin' but happy to be here with you. I'm not upset or let down, and as much as I might've seemed like I had plans to go crazy as soon as the door closed, I didn't. I'm not out of control over here, and one word from you, at any point, and we stop." He brushed a hand along my forehead, then tucked the hair that hung there behind my ear. "Tonight, let's just cuddle up in bed and read together, yeah?"

I nodded when he kissed my cheek and stood, seduced more by his words and his insistence I do, and say, and feel whatever I wanted than anything else he'd done so far. And of course, just when I wanted to jump him and at least enjoy him a little longer, he'd pulled back. My hesitancy had scared him off. I bit down on the irritation with myself and watched him wander into the bathroom.

He really didn't touch me again—not like that. He changed into shorts and a loose T-shirt and emerged with brushed teeth, then settled on his side of the bed. I took my turn, doing my best to ignore the critical nagging in my head, and focusing on the positives of the evening. We'd had a great dinner. We'd had great conversation. We'd had some great kissing, and then even more great communication.

So why did I feel like crying? What made me feel destroyed rather than triumphant? I didn't want to be in there consummating our marriage right this minute, but the shift from heat and touch to... reading and cuddling? It was too swift, and it'd seemed too easy for him.

Hadn't it?

I mean, he'd pinned me against the door and kissed my neck like he had plans, and now he sat out there, reading something on his e-reader like he'd never had anything else in mind.

But what could I say now? I balled the clothes in my hands and then dumped them in the laundry bag. I really needed to do laundry. I was down to my last pair of pajamas —a frilly little set with a spaghetti strap top and fluttery shorts made of the softest material in a light pink. Not ideal considering his immediate canceling of our physical interactions, because now I'd probably seem desperate or something. But I'd literally grabbed everything in my stack of pajamas that didn't have holes in it when I'd packed, and I'd officially plowed through every other option.

I crossed to the bed and noticed Noah had his e-reader smashed to his face.

"Uh, you okay?" I slid between the sheets and pulled the comforter to my waist, then leaned back against a pillow propped in front of the headboard.

"Mm-hmm." He didn't move.

"You sure?"

He pulled the book away and let it drop to the bed, then hit me with a look I'd call peeved. "Seriously?"

"Uh... yes? I do want to know you're okay."

He gripped the hair on either side of his head and rested his elbows on his knees. "I'm tryin' to be a good guy here."

I bit my lip to hide the smile and set a hand on one of his firm biceps. "You *are* a good guy. You're the best guy."

His whole body rose when his chest expanded, then he expelled a long, dramatic breath. Finally, he lifted his head and gazed over at me, then looked me over. His eyes traveled slowly and purposefully from my lips, down the slope of my neck, to the soft, thin tank top covering my chest, and back up.

When he spoke, his voice sounded strained. "Then maybe I was wrong, and you're not a very nice girl."

CHAPTER TWENTY-TWO

Noah

I'd never experienced the warring sensation of wanting to make love to someone while also wanting to strangle them.

Not *literally*, of course. But close. Because it'd taken every ounce of self-control and logic and goodness and *everything* to shift gears twenty minutes ago. It'd genuinely taken a lot out of me, but I'd escaped to the bathroom and given myself a good solid talking to about how I wouldn't go back out there and kiss her again. Not that if we did kiss, I'd lose all control and take things too far. I'd received the message that she wasn't there yet, and though I would've happily taken that step today, I understood.

And I wasn't about to be some jerk who took anything she didn't want to give. I'd promised myself that from the very beginning, and I wasn't about to start now.

But seriously? She walks out in *that* and I'm supposed

to, what? Just sit here and read my book like anything could hold my attention in the face of a living fantasy?

She'd poked and prodded until I said something, and now she was staring at me like she didn't know me at all. But I'd been thinking the same thing—maybe I didn't know *her* at all if she was cruel enough to walk out in that poor excuse for pajamas and expect me to ignore it.

"I'm nice." Her big brown eyes blinked back at me.

I just shook my head. Nope.

"How am I not nice?" She tilted her head to the side, and one strap of the top slipped down her shoulder.

I nearly groaned, averting my eyes, staring at the fascinating white ceiling. She couldn't be this oblivious, could she?

"Because you've essentially presented a diabetic with his favorite kind of chocolate cake. Or something' like that," I grumbled.

"And in this scenario, I'm the cake?"

My head snapped to see the wry smile on her face. I could hear it in her words, but seeing it sent lightning through me, white-hot need, and I gripped the sheets. My throat dried out, so I nodded.

There came the head tilt again, then a bite of her bottom lip just to add to the torture. "But if I'm the cake, and presumably you're the diabetic, that means I'd be bad for you."

She shook her head slowly, and *mercy, those eyes.*

I just watched. I didn't know where she was going with all this, but I'd fallen under her spell again and currently had no plans to attempt to break it.

She leaned on the hand closest to me. "You think I'd be bad for you, Noah?"

I cleared my throat. "It's not a perfect metaphor."

She cracked a smile and my chest tightened.

"I guess not. Especially because that would mean it'd never be good for you to enjoy the cake."

Pounding. Heart. Beating. I'd nearly lost sense as she spoke. Why had I ever used a damn metaphor? What was she saying? "What do you, uh, mean?"

She leaned closer. "I mean, in your scenario, there'd never be cake if we were going to avoid harming you. But I'm saying I think there should be cake—a whole cake at some point. And maybe a slice tonight, if you wanted it, but only if—"

My lips were on hers before she could finish the sentence. I'd never been so out of my mind with want, and I never would've dreamed talking about cake would prove to be the best seduction imaginable.

The next morning, when I woke, the world looked… brighter. Partly because we'd stayed up late into the night enjoying each other without doing everything, and we'd slept in. It'd been a long time since I'd slept this late outside the recent hospital stay.

I worried she'd be shy or clam up when she woke and saw me in the light of day. Not that I looked any different, but sometimes people got carried away at night. Neither of us had let the other get too carried away, but still.

Thankfully, she woke and brushed the hair out of her eyes, then grinned and rolled a little so she could hug me. She rested her head on my chest and let out a big sigh which I dared to interpret as contentment.

My heart ached at the thought, much like it had many times in the last few days. Even before I knew her well, I'd wanted to help her find happiness. The thought that she might find it with me…

"We need to talk about the retreat before we just show up there," she said quietly.

"You're right. I've been puttin' it off, but we have to check out here at eleven and check in over there at three. Let's head to breakfast and we'll go through it." I'd been avoiding talking about the retreat because that felt too much like a return to real life.

Here in this bubble world we'd created, where the care and intimacy between us were growing and our relationship felt like our own, felt like home. I didn't want to leave this place. Talking about the retreat would mean thinking about work and everything that came with that, including Allen's sniffing around the marriage.

And that brought it all home. Because it wasn't, and in four days, Katie would be hopping on a plane out of Munich and I'd stay here. The divorce papers were likely sitting in my mailbox back on post. It was all coming to an end just when it felt like we had a chance to start, and I didn't want to deal with that.

So I'd avoided it, but we couldn't do that anymore. At breakfast, we got down to business.

"I haven't been to a Strong Ties retreat, but I've heard about them. I think it's a lot of little icebreaker-type activities for the couples, and then there are sessions where they talk about more relationshippy-type stuff." I paused to take a bite of a delicious omelet. I'd miss the omelet station when we left.

"*Relationshippy-type stuff?* Is that a technical Army term?"

She bit into a strawberry, and I blinked away before I could get too distracted by the sight.

"Absolutely. Very official."

She chuckled. "Good to know."

"So we'll go through the sessions, though I told them we have to leave on Sunday before the last one. Your flight out is fairly early on Monday, and I don't want to be rushed back on post. If you don't mind, I want to hit up the mail-room and the commissary, and then I can make us dinner." And we can spend more time together.

Soak up every second before you leave. *Talk about you staying.*

That thought elbowed in, and though it surprised me in some ways, it felt inevitable in many others. I wasn't going to be able to return to regularly scheduled life after this. Maybe this weekend we could talk about other options. Maybe we could agree there were reasons to put things off a little and no reason to rush.

"I met a lot of people last week, but I'm afraid I won't remember many names. Colonel Wolfe, of course, and your friend Thatcher. But you said he's not married, so he won't be there, right?" She shoved a slice of melon around on her nearly empty plate.

"Sometimes they'll do a simultaneous event for single soldiers, and I do think they have one this weekend, but I'm not sure. If he is, then there'll be a few other friends there. Plus, you met Sergeant Major Allen, and he'll be very inter-ested in us." I gave her a meaningful look.

"Ah, okay. So. Anything I should know about our rela-tionship? Things you've told them about why I'm in the US, or... anything?" She held my gaze but pressed her lips together in a way that seemed nervous.

Of course she's nervous. Of course. She's about to be thrust into a situation where she knows no one but me, and it's not just a social engagement. It's a *marriage retreat.* I reached out with an open hand, and she immediately took it. My ribs ached, but not just where they were bruised.

"We'll be fine. I've been vague, mostly sayin' *it's complicated*. And the only other specifics I've given are that you got a great job right out of college and couldn't pass up takin' it, so you stayed there. That's all true."

Granted, if she'd really been my wife, I wouldn't have wanted to be separated at all. Ever. And if we'd had to make that our arrangement, I would've figured out a way to fly back to the States or have her come visit me every few months at least.

I wouldn't have been able to stay away. I would've wanted her with me like I did now. Like I would from now on.

Damn.

"That sounds reasonable enough," she said, then sat back and withdrew her hand.

"No one's going to be coming at us, tryin' to prove us false. In the end, they're going to want to see us together, and that'll be proof. It's not like everyone who's married is totally in love and getting along perfectly. A lot of people hate each other. I figure we're in pretty good shape at this point." I smiled, hoping for encouraging and lighthearted, even if dread pooled in my gut, and I wished I'd found a way out of this.

"Yeah, of course. We'll just act normal."

Right. Act normal. Be in love with my wife.

Not a problem at all.

CHAPTER TWENTY-THREE

Katie

I couldn't stop fidgeting. I knew I'd have to find some way to quell the nerves and not appear as uncomfortable as I felt. I had to. And not for me, but for Noah's sake. I didn't want to do anything that might get him in trouble or cause his bosses to be suspicious of us. We were so close to...

I shut my eyes against finishing that thought. After the last week, I didn't want to think about the end of things. I didn't want to dwell on the divorce. The closer it'd gotten, the less I'd thought about it, concertedly striking it from my mind. And that was before I got the call he had been captured. Now...

I could hardly stand to think of the last few days or last night. I sighed audibly, remembering his touch, his kiss, and my heart raced in response.

"You okay over there?" he asked from the driver's seat.

"Me? Yes, totally fine. Just nervous." Nervous, and

thinking about when we'll get to kiss again, but never mind me. That momentary distraction from the anxious twiddling of my fingers didn't take me anywhere near calm or particularly steady. Thinking about being alone with Noah made me feel breathless and excited in a way I'd never felt.

"You'll be fine. *We'll* be fine."

He sounded so confident that I hated myself for doubting. We'd gotten close over the last week. Maybe not *we've been married for five years* close. But everyone knew we'd been living apart, so it wasn't out of the norm that we didn't know every single thing about each other. *Right?*

We wandered around downtown Garmisch, an adorable little town full of small shops filled with gorgeous traditional Bavarian dirndls and lederhosen. There were outdoorsy stores and little restaurants flanking cobblestone roads and plazas. We ate lunch outside, the sun shining gloriously in the sky. And we laughed at all the funny interactions we'd had with Daniel, the bellman, but who also seemed to always be working and had startled us more than a few times by appearing out of nowhere to offer help.

The time in town proved to be the perfect distraction, and by the time we drove the five minutes to the military resort, Glockenblume, only mild anxiety and a decent pinch of sadness plagued me.

I couldn't ignore how soon I'd be leaving. The magic of our time alone had come and gone. I'd have to share Noah with other people, behave properly, and not just have him to myself. I hated the thought. I felt like I'd shared him with everyone else for so long—for five years. Now that I knew him, and knew how much I wanted him, I didn't want anyone else to have even a moment of his time.

Obviously, that wasn't possible. But as we settled our bags in the significantly smaller and less fancy hotel room with dark wood, slightly out of style curtains, an uphol-stered chair, and a bright white fluffy comforter on the queen-sized bed, I must've been making a face.

"I'm sorry it's a step down from the other room. I wish we could've stayed there these last few nights." He approached and set a hand gently on my arm.

"It's great. It's probably still the nicest room I've stayed in, if we don't count the last week." I smiled, but it felt false.

"That's not a real smile. Too bad for you, I've got you figured out by now." His eyes searched mine, stepping closer. "What's wrong?"

Could I tell him what I really thought? Not everything, for sure, but he'd genuinely asked. And I didn't want to be someone who had to be coaxed into talking about real things. I took a deep breath and willed myself to be brave and honest.

"I'm feeling selfish. I don't want to share you. I don't want to have to be cautious or think twice about what I'm saying. I guess I'm just a little sad we've left the dream world of the other place, but I'm glad we have a few more days together."

A few more days. My throat tightened at the thought, and I swallowed against the rise of panic that hit.

He ducked his head, and his arms came around me. He pulled me close and hugged me to him, speaking in that low, calming tone.

"We'll still have lots of time together. I'm pretty sure they give us date nights and all kinds of free time." He released me, then leveled me with his gorgeous blue eyes and continued. "Let's go check in so we'll have a schedule and know what to expect."

~

"Your breakfasts are included, but lunch and dinner are up to you. Please be on time for the sessions. We'll do our best to move through the material and get the most out of the time and then move on so you can enjoy everything Garmisch has to offer. Chaplain Rossi has great things planned for you. Questions?"

Lieutenant Colonel Wolfe answered a few questions, seeming patient and relaxed. I liked him. He'd dealt with me after receiving the worst news of my life, but he'd done it as well as could be expected, and he'd been faithful to check in every day, keeping me updated with what he was allowed to share. I'd been glad to meet him last week and looked forward to thanking him, again, for how he'd handled everything.

"Schedule looks pretty open. Just a few hours each morning, one afternoon session tomorrow, and some *mandatory fun* tonight." Noah spoke quietly next to me, the agenda in his hands.

"Seems good," I said, willing myself to perk up and enjoy the time. I refused to ruin the next few days with feeling sad and sorry for myself. I was always going to leave and nothing would change that. I had a job and a life to get back to, and so did Noah.

That thought, one I'd been less and less able to ignore, soured in my belly. *Ugh.* What was his life like? Did he date? Of course he did. I didn't really believe he was dating someone now, not actively, or it would've been pretty hard for him to convince people he was married faithfully. Though maybe that didn't matter to him.

I rejected that thought. Noah had integrity, and he wouldn't want to appear unfaithful. He couldn't very well explain our situation to everyone. But what did that leave? Dating apps or hooking up with random people?

I inhaled slowly and mentally grasped for calm. I counted, then visualized—tools I'd used to silence the loudest voices in my head over the years. Picturing Noah out in some European city meeting women made me want to vomit, but for some reason, the gates had been thrown open to that line of thinking.

"What's up?" he asked, grabbing my hand as we walked back to the room.

"Just thinking about the schedule and what we might want to do the next few days." My tone was bright. Maybe too bright.

His eyes narrowed and he studied me, but whatever he would've said never came because someone interrupted us.

"You guys made it! Great to see you." This came from a tall, extremely good-looking man I definitely remembered from the little meet-and-greet the week before. He was striking, yes, but he'd been so warm and kind, it'd made an impression.

"We did. Good to see you. Guess you're here for the single soldiers event?" Noah shook his hand.

"Yes, indeed. Doing a little babysitting, but also taking the time to visit Garmisch because it's awesome. Couldn't resist a chance to come enjoy it." He smiled and opened his arms wide, gesturing to the white walls and faded carpet.

"Well, we're off to get changed before dinner and some mandatory fun. I'm sure we'll run into you again." Noah took my hand in his.

"Of course. Have a great time. Nice to see you again, Katie." He held up a hand.

"You too, Thatcher," I said, sorry I couldn't remember his last name. Wilder? Something. He was nice and extremely handsome, so you'd think I'd be able to recall it. But with the nerves from being near Noah after the weeks that had led up to it, it wasn't a huge shock I hadn't been able to retain all that much.

We continued down the hall, then entered our room using traditional swipe-card style keys rather than actual metal ones. Somehow, these plastic versions seemed like the out-of-date ones compared to the metal keys at the resort, but that was likely because what lay behind the door at the other place was so gorgeous.

"He seems nice," I said as we entered the room and I dropped my purse on the edge of the bed.

Noah nodded. "Thatcher? Yeah. He's a great officer and a really good guy. Probably the nicest person I've ever met, actually. He's one of those people you just know is a quality person who helps people and cares about his soldiers. He's like a mini Colonel Wolfe in that way, I guess. But I know Wild a little better."

"That's great. I like knowing you have those kinds of people around you," I said, and though I didn't mean for it to come out the way it did, I could hear the soppy sad tone in my voice.

He took my hand and sat on the bed in front of me. Then he tugged me so I stepped closer, facing him and standing between his knees. His hands found my waist, and he held me in place, studying me.

I studied him right back, my heart rate accelerating at his touch, the position oddly possessive and thrilling, yet also comforting. Confusing, for sure. His face was serious— so serious, but so beautiful. My goodness, he was handsome. His blond hair was a little longer on top given he hadn't gotten it cut since before I'd seen him. His blue eyes and long, dark blond lashes, his thick eyebrows, sturdy nose, the jaw he'd shaved this morning, those lips...

I sighed and his eyes softened.

"I don't know what you're worried about, but I know it must be somethin' big. I want you to talk to me. Whatever it is, we'll handle it."

Oh, he destroyed me with that, and I couldn't hold back the rising sadness, the ache in my chest, or tears in my eyes.

"Katie, baby, please don't cry." He pulled me close and wrapped his arms around me, and I sank into the embrace.

My chest felt like it'd been sawed open, and everything was running out in violent gushes. Graphic, yes, but accurate. Because right then, in that moment, I knew. I knew it with a clarity I'd never experienced at any other time in my life except for when I'd fled the house and known I'd never go back the day I turned eighteen.

"Please talk to me," he whispered into my hair, desperation coloring his voice enough to make me pull back and press my hands to my face.

I took some gulping breaths, annoyed I couldn't calm down and just *speak*. But I settled enough to find my voice. "I didn't mean to cry. I'm sorry, I—"

"Stop apologizin' for your feelings. I don't care if you cry, even if it guts me. But I want to know how I can help." He tucked the hair behind my ear in a gesture now familiar. He did it whenever he wanted to soothe me or talked to me at close range and needed something to do with his hands.

I shuffled to the bathroom and wiped my face, blew my nose, washed my hands, and came back, inhaling slowly to calm myself. When I sat down next to him, he turned his palm up on his thigh, and I placed my hand in his.

I couldn't fully explain the crash of emotions just now, but I could start with one thing that'd been bugging me. One place my mind kept going. And though I hated it, I'd begun to wonder if he had the same concerns.

"This isn't why I was crying, for the record. But I have

been thinking about the people you date, and just found myself really envious of them. Getting to see you and be with you while I'm back in the States..."

His brows dropped low over his eyes. "The people I date?"

I nodded.

"Katie, are you askin' about people I've dated while we've been married?" He looked almost stricken.

And that was what I felt—stricken and hurt, probably undeservingly, over the prospect of him being with anyone but me.

He took my shoulders in his hands and dipped his head so we were close, eye to eye. It felt like minutes, but was probably only a few seconds before he asked, "Have you dated? Is that where this is comin' from?"

"No, never."

He dropped his head and shook it. "Why not? You're—you're gorgeous and smart and kind and—"

I laughed softly. "Thank you. But we're married. I wear my wedding band every day. I've never been with anyone while we've been together."

He crushed his eyes closed. "I never meant for that to be the way it was. I never wanted for you to be deprived."

I straightened and shook his arm. "Me? What about you?"

CHAPTER TWENTY-FOUR

Noah

I swallowed again. Why did this conversation make me so nervous? "What about me?"

"Have you dated? Or maybe not *dated* but," she frowned and looked slightly ill before saying, "hooked up with?"

"No."

Perplexingly, her frown deepened.

"Does that upset you?" Clearly, we'd needed to have this conversation. We both had loads of thoughts on the matter and had made lots of assumptions.

She huffed, and a lock of hair fluttered until she tucked it behind her ear. "It doesn't upset me, but it's hard to believe."

"You think I'd lie to you about that?"

She turned her wide brown eyes on me. "No, not really. Not unless..."

I nodded, urging her to finish the thought, my mind racing with the possibilities. Unless *what?* The thought she considered me capable of lying directly to her face about something like this unsettled me.

"Unless you thought it was for the best somehow, or more particularly, if you thought you were sparing my feelings or keeping me from being hurt."

Her posture had slowly deflated the longer she sat. She was practically hunched in half now, folded in on herself.

I shook her lightly on the shoulder until she sat up, waiting for her to meet my eyes before I spoke. "I have not dated anyone since we've been married. On the most practical level, it seemed sketchy, and I was concerned about bein' questionable when we were already doin' something unconventional. On a larger, much more important and personal level, I didn't like the idea of bein' with someone else while I was married to you—even if our marriage was superficial, let's say. I wouldn't lie to you if I had, because while I didn't feel good about it for me, I fully expected you to date other people."

She angled herself in my direction, opening her body and her whole demeanor to me. "But why? Why would you feel it was wrong for you to see someone, but acceptable for me? That makes no sense."

How could I explain this? "I wanted you to have a full, normal life. To begin to replace what you'd lost, or find what you'd never had growin' up. I wanted you to just *live*. And cuttin' out relationships isn't really that."

The room was quiet except for the distant patter of rushed footsteps somewhere above us. The hotel had several floors, and we were on the second, halfway between the main entrance and reception area and the last rooms, so we heard a lot of traffic in the hallways. I focused on that and wondered what occupied her thoughts. She kept her gaze on her hands for another moment before crossing them over her chest.

"I did live. I have. Maybe not by dating a bunch of guys, but I don't think I missed that much. I have good friends, I got a degree, and I have a job. Those are all things that have been satisfying and important to me."

"I hope I don't sound critical. I'm amazed by you. I truly am. And I hope it's not weird for me to say it, but I'm glad you didn't date anyone else."

A small smile tugged at the corner of her mouth. "Well, don't mind me saying so, but the selfish part of me is glad you don't have a whole stable of women waiting for me to get gone."

"Not a one."

"Good."

An hour after we'd entered, we emerged from the room, clothes changed for the evening and thankfully, on the same page. Neither of us had dated, and though it seemed unfathomable that she hadn't, I couldn't deny I felt victorious at the revelation. Victorious over what? I didn't quite know. But it felt like winning.

"So what is *mandatory fun?* I've heard you say that a few times over the years and twice tonight, so it must not just be a marriage retreat thing."

We held hands through the endless hallways of the hotel. It sprawled in what felt like every direction from the centralized lobby—our room was a full ten-minute walk from the main entrance on the second of four floors.

"It's any planned activity, really, but especially things

that are scheduled with an eye toward teambuildin' or icebreakin' or whatever. There are lots of mandatory fun activities in the Army life."

I'd often wished I had a date to take with me to things like Hail and Farewells and balls and organizational days. And at those times, I could admit to myself I wished the wife I had could be someone I interacted with. Or, at other times, I'd wish I wasn't married, so I could just find a date. Though, over the years, watching friends date and use apps, a part of me appreciated having an excuse to opt-out of all of that business.

"So dinner is considered mandatory fun?" She sounded understandably confused.

"Not usually, but somethin' Colonel Wolfe said about icebreaker games at the beginning has me thinkin' it's going to be a bit of that before we actually eat. The restaurant here is just a big American-style buffet with decent—not great—food."

I clasped her hand more firmly in mine, just a bit, then brought it to my mouth and kissed her knuckles. I'd never thought of myself as a PDA man, but I hadn't been an adult in a relationship before.

Odd thought, that. But it held true. I'd been a teen the last time I'd dated someone. And there again, another strange thing. *Were we dating? What were we doing?*

"Well, I'm not super hungry yet, so maybe the games will help us work up an appetite." She smiled and wiggled her eyebrows at me.

Lord forgive me, but I had ideas about other ways we could work up an appetite. Would I mention those now? No.

But honestly, after hearing we'd both chosen to be faithful to our sham marriage for years and years and *years,*

I'd wanted to just... go for it. All of it. Throw the divorce out the window, ask her to really be mine, ask her to move here and live with me and find a job and...

And give up everything she's worked so hard for.

That thought had stopped me from saying anything more, doing anything more. And as we approached dinner, I stood on a knife's edge, seconds away from dragging her back to the room. At the same time, I wanted to hide from her. I wanted to yell at Sergeant Major Allen for forcing me to bring her here, for putting us in the position of needing to perform like a married couple at all, and at myself for catching feelings in the first place.

"Join us over here, Miller." Speak of the devil who gestured us over.

"Katie, you remember Sergeant Major Allen, Colonel Wolfe, and his fiancée Livie?" I slid into the seat nearest Allen, and Katie followed after me.

"Great to see you again, Katie. How was the time at the resort? I've heard it's fabulous."

Livie's enthusiasm relaxed some of the tension ticking in my shoulders.

"It was gorgeous. We can't thank you enough for that gift. It was such a wonderful time for us."

She leaned into me, and my chest bubbled with the contact. With that *we*. I liked her talking about us as an *us*. I liked being with her in a *we*.

"I'm glad. The reviews sounded amazing, and I've driven by it a few times and thought it looked like a perfect couples retreat."

The way she said it made me think she'd had a pretty heavy hand in the location selection. I'd have to thank Colonel Wolfe again. Maybe Katie and I would write them a thank-you note.

"It was sort of like a honeymoon, honestly. We felt spoiled." She looked at me and bit her lip with a shy smile.

Oh, that smile did things to me. The idea of a honeymoon did things to me, too. Yes, we'd been spoiled, but if that had been our honeymoon? Yeah, I wouldn't have seen hardly any of the resort grounds.

"What did you do for your honeymoon?" Sergeant Major Allen's wife, Marcia, asked from where she sat next to him, across from Katie.

Katie's face looked panicked. I rubbed my hand along her back to comfort her and spoke. "We never had one. I deployed quickly after we married, so we just had a few nights in a hotel before I left."

All technically true. We spent a few nights in the Fort Campbell Army Lodging. But I didn't actually sleep in the hotel room then; instead, I returned to the barracks since I'd be helping her get settled and then leaving quickly after.

"That's a shame, but I'm so glad you had this time, even if the circumstances were unfortunate." Marcia's voice trailed off as she attempted to avoid addressing the awkward place this conversation had ended up.

I clenched my jaw, hating the embarrassment and shame that rushed in and filled my chest. Flashes of the week from hell I'd escaped only ten days ago now rattled in my mind.

"We are, too. Thank you all for making it happen." Katie's voice cut through the thoughts, and then she placed a soft kiss on my cheek.

The tension eased, and I clutched her to me, my arm around her back sliding her close so we were pasted together on the bench seat. It was the first time I'd given more than a few seconds' thought to the incidents that had caused all this, and I hadn't gone under with it. She'd pulled me out. She'd kept those thoughts at bay all week, for that matter. It made sense that being here, back with people from work and sitting with my bosses, would conjure the memories and the many feelings that came with them. But with Katie here, they didn't seem so overwhelming or inescapable.

CHAPTER TWENTY-FIVE

Katie

S leep eluded me.

The dinner had gone well... until it hadn't. We'd started on shaky ground, comments alluding to the events in Afghanistan throwing Noah into a different place. I hadn't seen him so serious, so visibly bothered, since before we'd left Kugelfels.

But was that a surprise? We'd left the dreamworld of the resort. We'd left the vacation haze of relaxation and feeding ourselves until we burst and the first kisses and contact of our relationship. Now we were surrounded by people from his job, which had created the circumstances that'd led to his capture and captivity.

I rolled to my side, smashing the pillow beneath my head. Noah had passed out when we got home. Any thoughts of physical intimacy had fled when the conversation about Captain Waverly had ended the evening. His recovery wasn't going very well. The mobility in his hand wasn't returning like the doctors expected, and these first few weeks were key. As Lieutenant Colonel Wolfe relayed the information, a dark cloud descended on Noah, and no amount of handholding or kisses on the cheek would remove it.

Not that I sat there like an idiot pecking his cheek, expecting that to solve the trauma and emotions undoubtedly pulling at him. On the walk back to the hotel room, which had seemed interminable, I'd asked if he was okay. He'd said yes, and explained that the conversation brought up a lot of the feelings he'd been able to put out of his mind the last week, and it seemed normal. He hadn't shut me out or gotten angry or refused to speak.

But he sounded, looked, and acted remote, his mind clearly circling the events of that week and worrying about his friend. He'd fired off a text to Captain Waverly, but Lieutenant Colonel Wolfe had mentioned he hadn't been very responsive, and not to worry if we didn't hear back.

No response came, at least not before Noah fell asleep. He'd curled up in bed after a shower. I had the fleeting, selfish thought that if it'd gone another way, I might've joined him in there. But that wasn't right tonight. I wished we were there in our relationship. I wished we'd built a foundation on which I could stand and hold him, carry him through some of this. Wasn't that what marriage was for? Supporting each other in the darkness—leading each other through, or sometimes clinging together, until you found the light?

Noah had fallen asleep but my mind, now hours later, wouldn't quit. I'd replayed every moment of the dinner, analyzing my own words and the questions and conversation around us. I'd thought through Noah's responses, wondered how I could help him, and sifted through everything I'd learned in my own therapy that might be of use to him.

What I couldn't avoid thinking about, though I'd attempted to distract myself from it with all of those other thoughts, were my feelings for Noah. Somehow, being surrounded by other people made me feel all the more acutely. And the reality settled in: my heart stood perilously close to falling completely for him. It'd be an irrevocable, unending kind of fall if I let it happen. I feared it, and yet so much of me wanted to throw my arms wide open and invite him in, let the emotion take over and join with the certainty I'd felt lurking at the edges of my mind that we belonged together. That we'd married five years ago for a more cosmic purpose than simply to help me escape my horrible family.

I heard a low sound from Noah, something pained and primal. Lightning struck my heart at the sound of it, fear and worry mingling. I turned and set a hand on his shoulder when the sound came again. He might've been speaking, but it came out mumbled and incoherent to my ears.

My hand on his shoulder broke through. He made no sound, but his eyes opened, wide and searching.

"Do you want light?" I asked, keeping my voice low and calm.

"Sure," he grunted out, sliding up so his back rested against the headboard.

I flipped on the lamp then turned back to find him ruffling his hand through his hair, his chest heaving with the labored breathing. I reached out to touch him, but before I made contact, he jerked the covers back and stood, then stormed to the bathroom. He didn't slam the door, which frankly surprised me considering the forceful exit from bed.

My mind raced while I waited, at first staying put under the covers, then standing to pace. I hadn't been sleeping anyway, but this had sent my heart pounding and my mind scattering in all directions. How could I help him? What did he need?

Minutes later, he emerged from the bathroom. He walked, markedly calmer, and in a swift movement, shucked his T-shirt and pitched it into his suitcase. The light *thwap* of the shirt against the back of the bag sounded loud in the room. No footsteps or distant conversations filled the air. At two in the morning, it seemed most people had retired for the night.

He turned to me with his hands on his hips but didn't look up at me. He seemed consumed by his thoughts, like he needed to decide something before he could look me in the face or talk to me. I couldn't read his mood anymore. He was no longer angry or frustrated, but he definitely wasn't ready to climb back into bed and sleep.

I kept my eyes averted. The removal of the T-shirt bared his beautiful chest, and it didn't seem right to appreciate his pose in just shorts or notice the way his hands at his hips highlighted the tightly stitched patchwork of his abs. I shouldn't be ogling my husband in his time of need.

"Thank you for wakin' me," he said, low and gruff. His gaze finally met mine, the look in his blue eyes incomprehensible.

"I'm sorry you're not sleeping well." I almost said *I'm sorry you had a bad dream*, but I knew how inadequate of a term *bad dream* was for the kind of terrors that our minds could conjure.

He exhaled loudly, and his hands dropped to his sides.

"I hadn't been. I've had some of the best sleep of my life the last week." Something in his face made my stomach drop. "I think being surrounded and talkin' about Waverly just set my mind on that track."

I sat on the bed and reached out a hand. "You know I understand. Any idea what would help? Do you want to talk about it?"

He joined me on the bed and took my hand, his focus there when he spoke. "Not really. It's normal to have dreams, I know that. It's normal to have feelings and guilt and shame and all of that. I'm ready to just put it all behind me, and I'm frustrated that I haven't. But I get that it's not somethin' that happens magically in a week. Even if it was a great week." He squeezed my hand, then brought it to his lips and kissed the back of it.

I loved that he did this. He did it a lot, almost like he couldn't help but kiss me and show affection in some way. My heart fluttered and ached for him, knowing he was in the midst of processing what had happened.

"I'm sorry. I wish there was a shortcut."

A half-smile crept to his lips. "Yeah, me too."

We sat in silence, both of us lost in thought until my body felt heavy and my mind slowed enough to consider sleep. I wondered if he'd be able to sleep at all and desperately wanted to help him the way he'd done for me.

"I don't know if you want to sleep. But if you do, I could..." I trailed off, suddenly breathless with nerves.

He raised his brows in question, waiting for me to finish my thought.

"I could hold you. Like you did for me." I swallowed, frustrated with myself for feeling nervous to suggest this. He'd held me after my nightmare just days ago. Why should it make me anxious now? If he didn't take me up on the offer, it didn't mean he rejected me.

In response, his face changed—his brow dipped low, almost like my offer pained him. But he cleared his throat, and his, "Yes, please" sounded like it took all the energy in the world to speak the words.

I didn't know what to make of it, but he'd said yes, and he was moving, sliding down between the sheets. I expected him to turn away from me so I could wrap my arms around his back and hold him like he had me. But instead, he faced me, his eyes flickering all over me.

My breath moved shallow in my chest as I slipped lower and rested my head on the pillow and then reached for him. He eased closer. I slipped an arm under his head and placed the other over his side. We lay like this for a moment, but then he chuckled.

"I don't think I can sleep like this. Your arm will be numb in five minutes with my fat head weighin' it down."

The humor in his voice was pure music. He'd recovered enough to joke, and that let the tightness in my chest ease a bit.

"Okay, well, how do you want to..."

He jostled around a bit, guiding an arm here, a hand there. When he was done, I lay with my head on his chest and shoulder, his arm under my head, my leg hitched up and over both of his, and my arm over his ripped stomach. I promised myself not to give in to the temptation to stroke his abs or enjoy his current shirtless state.

"Can you grab the light?"

I looked up when he glanced down, and our faces nearly touched. My heart thundered in my chest, but I answered instead of giving in to the pull to press my lips to his. "Yes."

I leaned away and reached for the lamp, found the switch, and curled back into him. I rested my head on him and listened to his heart, which sounded like it beat in a sprint like mine. After another minute, his ribs expand beneath me and I heard a long sigh.

I jumped slightly when he rested his free hand on my leg where it lay across his, but eventually, I let out my own sigh. His palm seemed hot. In fact, all of him did. There was no way I'd be able to sleep like this, the smooth skin of his chest burning under my cheek.

I lay there, my heart still running too fast considering I just lay there, not moving, not exerting in any way, snuggled into him. But it also hurt—it ached. Seeing him so frustrated, then accepting. It piled up more pieces of him I found appealing. He didn't complain or rage or freak out, though if he had, I couldn't have blamed him. He'd seemed resigned but not defeated. He had such an amazing balance of determination and calm, like he knew panicking, or crying, or having a good old-fashioned tantrum just wouldn't make any difference.

I wished I could be more like that, but I'd learned my coping mechanisms the hard way. Long years, lots of therapy, and I still had to fight sometimes. Laying here with Noah, though, wasn't a fight. At least, not that kind.

It was the skin that did it, if I had to pin it down. The curve of his pectoral, and the warmth and slow stroke of his thumb over my thigh where his hand rested. They pushed all thoughts from my mind until I turned my face to his skin and kissed his chest.

His breath hitched and he stilled, but the hand on my leg gripped me and pulled me close. I kissed him again, an inch from the first. Then again.

Faster than I could've imagined, he was over me, his

mouth on mine, and nothing had ever felt better, more right. Every part of me lit up with energy and expectation. So much so that I wouldn't have been surprised to find myself glowing under him.

This was it. Finally. Years in the making, I sank beneath him as he claimed my mouth, claimed *me*, just as he should.

CHAPTER TWENTY-SIX

Noah

My wife still slept next to me, and my head swam with the memories of the night before.

The next breath I took was slow and deep while I savored the sight of her. Her brown hair spilled around her, hiding half her face. She slept curled up like she had every other night, as though she needed to take up as little space as possible. If you saw her and didn't know, you'd think she was small, unassuming. Not a threat.

But the last few weeks had revealed to me a new kind of danger, and here she lay dormant beside me. My heart felt too big, too full to fit inside me anymore as I watched the subtle movement of her body when she breathed. She'd comforted me on so many levels last night, and yet this morning, I felt utterly destroyed.

My breath felt thin and inadequate. I needed space.

I moved silently from the bed, hoping I wouldn't wake

her, and escaped to the bathroom. I splashed water on my face, brushed my teeth, then braced myself on the counter and looked into the tired eyes staring back at me.

"Get a grip, man." I spoke quietly to myself, still mindful of Katie sleeping in bed.

Just the thought of her made me ache and burn. I wanted her again, and I wanted to disappear. Because far more than the physical desire for her, which burned magma hot, was the reality I could no longer deny. I loved her. I was in love with her. And I didn't know what to do with that.

Tell her, you idiot.

It'd been on the tip of my tongue throughout the night last night, even before we'd made love. And that's what it had been, undoubtedly. If I thought it was that simple, I would just say it. But the words from my therapist punched in when I imagined pouring out my feelings at her feet and begging her to stay. *Try not to make any big decisions for a while.* He'd emphasized how post-traumatic decision-making can be skewed. That it was best to stay the course toward whatever one already had planned rather than changing plans. It made sense.

So would it be irresponsible to derail the arrangement we'd always had, always agreed upon, to divorce this summer? It felt wrong to barrel toward that without checking the plan against the experiences we'd shared. Not just bad, not just scary or sad, but actively *wrong*.

I straightened, standing tall, giving my reflection a determined nod. I didn't know how she felt, but I could broach the subject. We didn't have to change everything all at once. We didn't have to have all the answers. But I'd be a fool to let fear keep me from having the conversation.

～

The morning session was nearly through. My attention faded in and out after I'd lapsed into a sugar coma—the result of the pancakes I'd wolfed down at breakfast, and then the donut I'd eaten during an icebreaker game for the morning session. I should've been taking notes, doing whatever I could to pick up the advice the chaplain and speaker were sharing about marriage. Because I'd realized I wanted a real one, and I had no idea how to navigate that.

But instead, I kept becoming distracted by Katie—both the Katie next to me and the potential future Katie. My actual wife, maybe the mother of my children, maybe my traveling partner and lover, and the person I said good night and good morning to.

"Did you finish?" She tilted her head to look at the packet of papers in front of me on the conference table.

"Yes, ma'am, I did." I tapped the pen against the paper with a nod. We'd taken a test to identify how we communicated and received love. I'd never thought about it before, but my answers made sense. I couldn't wait to hear what hers were, too. Then I could love her better. More significantly than all the ways I wanted to show her in my own mind, but also through channels that she would receive more potently.

"So, what'd you get for giving? How do you give love?" She crossed one leg toward me, the toe of her shoe brushing my shin.

My stomach flipped. Did this even matter? Didn't we need to go back to the room?

I cleared my throat. "Uh, looks like physical touch was my way of giving."

Her lashes fluttered, then she bit her lip and a warm flush crawled up her neck as she nodded. "Makes sense."

Not sure what that meant, but okay. The lip biting and

blush seemed like it was probably a good sign. Or, the thought embarrassed her. "And you?"

"My ways of giving were tied—verbal affirmation and acts of service. What about how you receive love?" She met my eyes again.

I smothered a grin. "Also physical touch."

Instead of another blush like I'd anticipated, her brow furrowed and chin ducked. "Ah. Mine's acts of service."

"All right, folks, that's it for today's morning session. Keep talking with your partner while you enjoy lunch, and we'll see you back at three." The chaplain dismissed us, and people sprang out of their chairs, everyone ready to get out and enjoy part of the day before we had to return.

Her response nagged at me as we wound our way through the conference side of the hotel back toward the main lobby. We'd planned to go into town for lunch but had to swing by the room first.

"Miller." The voice stopped me mid-stride.

"Yes, Sergeant Major?"

Allen stood there, his perpetual frown a bit deeper. "You talked to Dr. Wagner in the last three days?" He crossed his hands over his barrel chest.

I glanced at Katie, who studied me, then I spoke. "Uh, no, I haven't. I—"

"Call him today. You're supposed to check in with him every seventy-two, and you know it."

"Roger. Will do. I'll call him right now."

Allen squinted at me, but nodded, then turned and tromped back over to his wife, who I now saw stood waiting for him about twenty feet farther down the hallway.

"You haven't been talking to your therapist?" Katie's voice was quiet but grated all the same.

"We've been a little busy, and I've been fine. But I'll

take ten minutes and check in when we're back at the room, okay?"

The edge in my tone shouldn't have been there. It wasn't her fault. None of it was. She was the goodness, the peace, the relief. The beauty in these last few weeks. And I didn't want her to feel bad for asking me. But Allen's abrasive approach and knowing he was monitoring me due to both the capture and his suspicion about my marriage made me want to hit something.

We walked silently, and notably not holding hands, to the room. The ten-minute walk felt like thirty, but we made it. I stepped out on the balcony and connected the call. The phone rang and I closed my eyes, inhaled the cool mountain air, then slumped into one of the cheap, plastic patio chairs and tried to calm my thundering heart.

"How are you, Noah?" Dr. Wagner's voice came through, soothing and familiar. He didn't sound angry or irritated like Allen had, and that went a ways toward relaxing me.

"Sorry I haven't called."

"You've been busy."

I nodded. "I have. It's been... A lot has happened."

I could hear him shifting around, maybe in a leather chair or something. "Tell me about that."

"No issues until last night. I had a dream. But otherwise, I've barely thought about it." I shifted in discomfort at the memory of the dream, then waking disoriented in the bed to Katie's hand on my shoulder.

"Why, do you think?"

"I'm sure it's because we're down at the resort. It's not just Katie and me anymore. Now I'm surrounded by people from work. And then they told me about Waverly's hand. I just had it all sink in, and I couldn't ignore it anymore, I guess."

"Sounds likely. Am I hearing that you've been attempting to ignore thoughts of the event?"

I ran a hand through my hair.

"Yes and no. I've been enjoyin' life. I've been," I swallowed "fallin' in love with my wife. So it wasn't that I made a point to avoid certain thoughts, it just slipped away in the context of so much good stuff."

"That does sound like good stuff. You don't sound particularly happy about it. Tell me about that."

I shook my head at the phrase I'd now heard a hundred times in the few meetings we'd had. "Hard to explain, but we're plannin' on divorcing this summer. This whole thing has thrown that into question. I don't—"

I stopped and gazed out at the mountains. They were covered in green, the spring bringing to life every little growing thing right up to the snowline.

"Go on."

I sighed. "You said I shouldn't make any big decisions."

"I did say that. I believe it to be sound advice."

I stood and leaned on the balcony banister. "I get that. So does that mean I shouldn't be divorcing her? Or I shouldn't be *not* divorcing her?"

A pause. "I can't tell you that, particularly without talking about the dynamic of your relationship which you have declined to speak about. What I can say is that you could take a middle road and communicate with your wife. Find out how she feels. Know that your own feelings may be heightened or blunted by the experience in Afghanistan, but that doesn't mean they are false."

"So you're not going to tell me what to do?" I joked.

"That's not really my job, Noah."

"I know." I blew out a breath. "Does this count as a good check-in? I don't want to seem like I'm avoiding talkin'—it helps. And I have an appointment for Monday afternoon. If it's okay with you, I'll just plan to talk to the local guy then."

He confirmed he found the plan acceptable, then hung up. I stayed outside another few minutes, attempting to gather my thoughts. Katie and I needed to talk, and there was no time to lose.

CHAPTER TWENTY-SEVEN

Katie

We obviously had some heavy conversations coming based on the look Noah gave me, and I assumed we'd do that at lunch. But then we ran into a group from the conference, and having any truly personal conversations became out of the question. Everyone chatted across tables. They were doubles but situated so closely side by side that in order to sit down, the server pulled the table out and then pushed it back into place once the person on the booth side was seated.

"So Katie, what do you do?" Livie asked from *right* next to me.

I'd seen Noah's face when the server led us to the table, the only one left on this busy late spring weekend. It was right next to Lieutenant Colonel Wolfe and Livie. He liked the man, but we certainly couldn't talk about our marriage there.

"I'm a teacher."

"What? Me too! What grade?" She patted my leg.

"Kindergarten," I said, smiling at her enthusiasm.

"Seriously? Me too!"

From there, we launched into a detailed conversation about our curriculum and swapped stories and ideas. We'd both only taught kinder for a few years, and we both loved it. She had a decade-plus more experience than I had, so I asked her questions and wished we could spend more time together. I wondered what it'd be like teaching all military kids who moved around all the time. I liked that once I moved to administration, I'd get to know all the kids, and see them grow older. I shared that thought with Livie.

"I have loved teaching, but about six months into my first year, I realized my place is in administration. I'm starting a master's program at Duke in August, so it'll be different to not start back with a new kinder class in the fall. It definitely makes me sad." I felt the pang of sadness mixed with excitement. The change would be bittersweet, for sure.

"I don't envy you the switch to administration, but we need people who are passionate about the students to be there. As DODEA teachers, we'll get kids for a few years and they always come visit their classrooms. We'll have that for a year or so, but then they move on. I can't imagine getting to see kids grow up all the way through elementary." She sounded a little wistful, and her fiancé grabbed her hand. She beamed back at me, clearly not *too* sad about the situation.

"Yeah. I can only imagine seeing my former kinder kids grown to be big fifth or sixth graders. It seems unfathomable, but at the same time, I love the idea of longevity in a place. I feel like it makes being in education in one place very special." I pressed the napkin in my lap and smiled at her.

She smiled back, agreeing with gusto at what a privilege that would be. All the while, I noticed Noah was curiously quiet. He wasn't typically gregarious or anything, but he usually piped in to ask a question, especially when I talked about teaching. Maybe he was still concerned about the call with his therapist, but it might've also been that he was sitting next to his boss.

Because of the crowded restaurant, we didn't get out of there until fifteen to three. We had to race back to the hotel to make the next session time. In the car on the short drive, I broke the silence.

"I'm sorry we couldn't talk at lunch."

He shot me a look with a small smile. It didn't quite reach his eyes, but it seemed better than the somber look he'd had all day. "Not your fault, Katie. You don't have to apologize for that. We'll have time tonight."

The afternoon session focused on communication. It was well-timed, obviously, except we still couldn't have in-depth conversations in this crowded space. In theory, everyone was tuned in to their own situations and not paying attention to anyone else. But I wasn't about to bring up the original dynamic of our marriage or how it'd changed. Or how I wanted it to change.

I hated to feel ungrateful, but as the chaplain led us through the little workbook, I felt antsy, like if I didn't get out of there soon, I'd have to excuse myself and take a break anyway. Noah didn't say much, and he seemed preoccupied and less talkative than I'd come to expect.

My contemplations of the best exit strategy occupied me while anxiety and frustration along with a healthy dose of curiosity crawled up my neck. Nearing a point where I'd need to stand and excuse myself, the chaplain clapped his hands, then held them up.

"I'm all through here for today. Great job, everyone. Have a great date tonight, and I'll see you back here after breakfast tomorrow for one last session."

I must not have been the only one itching to escape because several people rocketed out of their seats and made for the doors. Noah stood, grabbed my hand, and we were off, practically flying down the hallway. I clutched my purse and the books we'd been working through in the other hand, trailing him.

We didn't speak on the walk to the room, so I used the time to gather my thoughts, even with his hurried pace. My heart pounded its bass drum beat that I couldn't help but feel was remarkably foreboding, but it had to be because we were practically jogging through the hallway.

By the time the latch clicked shut on the door, I felt frantic. The anxious need to escape piled up with Noah's silence, the obnoxious mute march to the room all filled my belly with cement.

He paced the room. I sat on the edge of the bed and waited, my pulse racing. Finally, he stopped, hands on his hips, and pinned me with a stare. After a few blinks, his face softened, and he scrubbed a hand from his hair down over his eyes, then sat next to me.

"How would you feel about tabling the conversations and just goin' out for some fun tonight?" He laced our fingers together.

I had most definitely not expected that. I'd been feeling like a child about to be scolded, or someone about to get really bad news. And here he sat offering to push that conversation away, whatever it would be, and just enjoy this place?

"If you're sure." I didn't want thunderous, silent Noah. I wanted talkative, sweet, interesting, adorable Noah.

He kissed the back of my hand. "I'm sure. My mind is numb from the retreat, and I just want to get out and do somethin' fun. We'll have to head back fairly early tomorrow, and thank the Lord we have a valid excuse to skip the mornin' session. So this is our last chance to make a memory."

I swallowed when he said that and dropped my chin when I felt my eyes sting. What a terribly final thought—our last chance to make a memory. My ribs must've tightened around my lungs because it was suddenly quite hard to take a breath. But he wanted to get out and live another few moments together, and I wanted that too. I did want more memories with him, even if the thought of this being the last one felt like I'd been cut open.

I blinked rapidly, dismissing the tears, and found a smile for him. It wasn't so hard to smile at him because I loved him. I wanted him to have all my smiles, and I wanted his. Our time together barreled toward a close so quickly—absolutely bearing down on us with no way to escape—and I couldn't change that.

But we could go out and take this time. And we could deal with whatever dreadful conversations we had to in the morning.

∾

Noah moved as though on a mission when we left the room. We nearly jogged through the hotel, then zipped through town to park at the old Garmisch-Partenkirchen Olympic Ski Stadium. It was such a cool place in itself. But we blazed around it and up a long road until we arrived at a small hut where he doled out euros and we entered a path.

"What's a *klamm?*" I wondered aloud, assuming it meant path or some kind of hike. Large trees lined the paved trail that led up one side of a river.

"It means gorge. This is the *Partnachklamm* or the Partnach Gorge. We won't make it very far before closing. We should've come here earlier or last week. I didn't want you to miss it."

He grabbed my hand and off we went through a small, wet hole in the side of the stone. We disappeared into utter darkness as we carefully moved through the little passageway to the other side then out onto a thin path that snaked its way along the river that'd cut through the stone.

It absolutely stole my breath. Even in the waning daylight, the water glowed a vivid blue and rushed in some places but flowed almost calmly in others. The water had carved the stone walls of the gorge over centuries. It was like each lap of the river against the hardness left a mark, the delicate swirls and waves in the stone looking painted on.

We stopped on the trail where the rock curved in a dramatic half-circle. We hadn't seen anyone else on the path, and it felt like we were completely alone there. Noah had held my hand on and off. Sometimes the way proved too narrow, and most of it we'd walked single-file. But now, he turned to me with a look that caused an ache in my throat and a thump in my chest.

His eyes were serious and his gaze filled with wonder from the same awe I'd been feeling while inspired by the beauty around us. But he directed it at me. He brought a hand to the side of my face and his thumb brushed lightly over my cheek. He didn't speak or kiss me. He just looked at me.

His attention made me feel special and cared for, but something in his face sent a jolt of alarm through me. I couldn't tell exactly what, but it seemed... final. Eventually, his hand dropped, and he turned back to the path. So I did too, clutching my water bottle and gulping down swallows like it would solve the problem of my aching heart or my scrambled mind.

After just forty-five minutes, we were directed by a man sweeping the trail to turn around. We did so, following behind him dutifully. I tried to enjoy the return trip, but a sharp sense of loss permeated my thoughts.

We hadn't seen the whole thing; we hadn't had enough time. I wanted to see it all. I wanted to go all the way through and then take the more difficult hike back. I wanted hours there. Noah had mentioned there were other gorges he'd been to. He mentioned a trip to the gorge during winter when icicles dressed the walls.

I would never see those things. And somehow, this beautiful place had become a symbol not only of my time here, which was essentially over, but also of the end of my marriage. After all the things we'd started here—building emotional and physical intimacy, truly coming to know each other. And now we'd run out of time. We'd never get to really experience them, not the way we should.

By the time we returned to the hotel, my mournful mood had fully taken hold. If Noah noticed, he didn't mention it.

"Let's get pizza and stay in tonight. I'm worn out."

I didn't look at him to respond, fearful any prolonged looking at him would cause the dam to burst. "Sounds good. I'm just going to hop in the shower."

I shuffled into the bathroom and let the warm water soothe me for a moment before I broke down. I didn't want this to be it—our last night here, and my last real night in Germany. Tomorrow night would be awful, knowing it would truly be my final night with him. Plus, my flight left early, and he said we'd need to leave several hours prior, so we'd depart at something like five in the morning. There wouldn't be time—no lingering in bed whispering together or relaxing over coffee.

No more chances.

CHAPTER TWENTY-EIGHT

Noah

She'd grown quiet since lunch, but then I'd done the same. I couldn't blame her, even if I wanted to push her into telling me what thoughts occupied her so completely.

Wasn't that the most annoying thing? When someone you love and want to know everything about won't just slice themselves open and serve up every thought and detail on a platter? How dare she.

I'd dragged her to the gorge for distraction—selfishly. I couldn't sit in this room and stare at a woman I loved, but whom I'd realized had an entire life without me.

You'd think that would've been obvious considering we'd lived apart for five years. But somehow, her telling Livie about her teaching and plans to see her former students grow... it had clicked. I'd finally realized what a futile hope I'd been nurturing with daydreams of her moving here.

What a fool.

And yet, I didn't want to waste our time. So I'd chosen a distraction I should've taken her to sooner because it felt like a truly special place. But something happened to her. She'd chatted on and off on the walk, but on the way down, it was like she pulled down the curtains and locked the doors. Like there was no one home for me anymore.

I couldn't bear the thought of stumbling upon someone from work and having to share her, even if I had no idea how to manage all the feelings fighting for my attention. I wanted to ask her what was wrong. I wanted to kiss her and make love to her. I wanted her to leave *right now*.

I wanted to beg her to abandon her life, her students, her apartment, her friends, her *everything*, and be with me.

I let out a harsh breath while unlocking the door, pizza in hand. Mercifully, my favorite local Italian restaurant would deliver food to the side gate of the hotel. Gates surrounded the grounds, and it stood on part of a small compound guarded the same way the more typical military bases were, so most restaurants couldn't drive onto the property to deliver to the lobby. But the back gate was a secret of sorts, and I thanked God for it as I smelled the tomato sauce and warm crust.

Katie stood in front of her suitcase, her back to me when I entered. Instead of mentally cataloging my big fat feelings on the walk to get the pizza, I should've been planning how to handle the room tonight. I refused to waste the time together, even though we'd both taken steps away, moving us notably apart in the last few hours.

"Not sure if you like action or not, but I grabbed a DVD

from the lobby." I held up *True Lies*, hoping it could assist with distraction.

She turned toward me, her lovely face clean of makeup and her eyes a little red. Had she been crying? The thought took my heart in its fist and squeezed mercilessly. I set the pizza on the desk and moved to her.

"What's wrong? Please tell me, baby." The endearment slipped out without thought. Whenever it did, it felt natural. It *was* natural now.

She smiled, but it seemed pasted on since her eyes were still notably sad. "I'm fine. Just a lot of... big feelings, as we say in kindergarten."

I grabbed her hand and tugged so she'd face me fully, musing at my own use of a similar phrase moments ago. She kept her gaze downcast until I nudged just under her chin. When she met my eyes, her lips were smashed together, like she was holding something in. My pulse took off, wondering if this could be an in to talk about the laundry list of subjects we needed to cover before she left.

"Please talk to me. What big feelings?"

She took a steadying breath and stepped back but thankfully began to speak. "This has been a lot. Being here with you. In one way, it started out so intense with the hospital and seeing you again after everything. And then the rest has been intense in another."

She looked past me, out the glass doors to the balcony.

"It has been intense, for sure." To put it mildly. I would definitely be dealing with the experiences of the last few weeks for months to come. And in reality, amazingly enough, it might not be the capture that left the biggest impression.

"So I'm just kind of overwhelmed, I guess. It's nothing

to worry about. Sometimes, you just need a good cry. I guess it was time for me to have one." She flashed a smile, then stepped all the way out of my space. "Should we eat? I don't want the pizza to get cold."

I let her off the hook. Digging around in my own *big feelings* didn't appeal to me, so I couldn't very well expect her to elaborate. I didn't have the energy to navigate my own heavy heart, the sense of inevitability that'd struck early today while she spoke about her job, and the genuine sadness at the end of her visit.

So, we sat in bed and watched *True Lies*, the ridiculous story wringing out laughs. We shared smiles as we both functioned in an oddly somber mood considering we were having pizza and a movie in bed. Later, she fell asleep, tipped to the side on a pillow we'd used for an armrest between us, and I reluctantly found sleep an hour later.

Sometime in the night, we reached for each other, taking solace without words.

We'd extricated ourselves from the hotel, the retreat, and sadly, the city of Garmisch. Every kilometer we traveled away from the mountains, the heavier the weight on my chest grew. Somehow, we made light chitchat, commenting on someone we saw on the way out of the hotel or pointing out an interesting something or other out the window. Somehow, I kept myself from slamming on the brakes, pulling her from the car, and begging her not to go.

Because I desperately wanted to do just that. I didn't want her to leave. But I knew she had to go. On the most practical level, she'd taken leave from her job and they were expecting her back. Oh, and then the master's program news which, somehow, we'd never discussed. How had we missed that?

And on every other level, we'd planned to divorce. We'd always planned to go our separate ways—even more separate—and I couldn't throw that plan to the wolves because I'd been captured by the bad guys.

No. Absolutely not. It wasn't fair to her, either. She'd blown up her life to get here, to stay here and maintain this hoax so Allen and his obsession wouldn't end up costing me my career. She didn't need guilt hanging around her neck when she flew home.

So I kept my damn mouth shut. Probably more than I should've. And even as I did, I hated it. I wanted to talk with her and feel close to her, not set up this distance between us like I had time to burn and didn't mind wasting it.

By the time we got to Kugelfels a few hours later, I nearly dove out of the car. I needed space from her, or I'd end up saying something to overwhelm her. I pulled into the community mailroom lot and said, "I'll just be a second," then jumped out and jogged inside. I'd already decided not to deal with groceries. We'd eat from whatever I had in the cupboards, and I'd go tomorrow. It was something else to occupy my time once she left.

The contents of my mailbox turned out to be mostly forgettable—a bit of junk mail that had somehow found me, a letter from my bank, and a large manilla envelope from my lawyer.

I held it away from my body like it might poison me, and I would've tossed it to the floorboard on the passenger side if Katie hadn't been sitting there.

"Can I hold that stuff for you?"

She reached for the stack, but I held them tight for just a moment before releasing it to her. "Sure, yeah. Thanks. Nothin' special there."

Except for the divorce papers. Except for the thing that would dissolve any connection between us for good.

CHAPTER TWENTY-NINE

Katie

His face looked ashen when the desk attendant declared there were no rooms available at the Kugelfels lodging, period.

"I'm so sorry. We can head into town and see if we can get somethin' there, but we're on the early side of the summer PCS cycle, and I'm afraid—"

"Noah, it's not your fault. It didn't occur to me either, and we've had other things going on. I can crash on your couch or... wherever. This way, we save money, too."

I tried for an encouraging smile, but I hadn't felt much like smiling—not since yesterday. Today had been another exercise in the surreal. Leaving Garmisch and all of his work colleagues, returning to the military base and a place we'd been *before*. Before we'd gotten to know each other, spent nearly all day every day for a full week together.

Before I'd fallen in love with him.

His barracks apartment was close to the lodging building. We drove just a block or two and he parked. By the time he opened the door to his room, he'd apologized so many times, I wondered what I was about to walk into.

The simple space with utilitarian furniture looked, if not homey, then comfortable, and nothing alarming caught my eye. The efficiency kitchen looked tidy, the place probably cleaned before he'd left for Afghanistan. I couldn't imagine he had come home last weekend and cleaned after being in the hospital.

"It's not much, but it's home for now." His voice came out rough and unsure.

"It's great. Maybe a tad smaller than mine, but not by much." I smiled again, that same sticky, odd smile I kept lobbing at him in an effort to make him feel better. Or make me feel better? But anytime I did it, he looked more disturbed. I needed to try it out in the mirror and see what kind of damage I was doing.

"If you're okay with it, we can share the bed. Or, of course, I can take the couch and you can—"

"We've shared a bed every night of the last seven, Noah." *And we've made love several times.*

I didn't add the last part. It wouldn't be helpful. We'd gone from married and in love—or at least acting like it, and definitely feeling it on my part—to separate and awkward in the matter of a three-hour drive.

I hated the distance between us, but I didn't know how to repair it. It'd been growing, and even though we'd both reassured each other that we had the time and could just be together, we'd lied to ourselves.

He ripped into his mail, one after another, then tossed the pile onto his desk almost angrily. I focused on reviewing my ticket information, confirming I had my passport accessi ble, and messaging Sarah to see if she could still drop my car off at short-term parking so I'd have it.

We ate dinner at the small table in his living room slash kitchen, some pasta and jarred sauce he had in his pantry, and after, he stationed himself at the sink to do dishes. "I'll just get these done and then grab a shower. Then you can take your time in there, okay? I don't think you want to leave it to the morning."

I nodded, feeling so many things at once, I couldn't speak. I wandered around his apartment while he showered, inspecting the cupboards where he stored dry goods, eyeing the coffee maker, and noting the contents of his freezer.

He had a few books on the shelf next to his bed, and most surfaces seemed clean. His desk reflected the same orderliness, except for the mail he'd thrown. I shouldn't have, but I edged closer, first admiring the photo of his mom with her forehead against the muzzle of her horse. She was such a lovely woman, and a pang of sadness rushed through me at the thought of losing her, too. She checked on me about once a month, always insisting she didn't want to pry. And now, after all this, after *me* being the one to come out here...

I pushed those thoughts away, determined to maintain at least some contact with her. Even if Noah and I lost touch.

The prospect of never speaking to Noah, not even in the superficial ways we had in the past, knocked me forward. I leaned on the desk, bracing against the pain the thought caused.

My eyes moved to the messy pile of half-opened mail under my hands. Just a glance sent any shred of hope I'd had left plummeting. *Petition for Dissolution of Marriage.*

My stomach clenched, and my mouth watered like I might throw up.

I gritted my teeth, grabbed my purse, and ran for the door. I needed air, space, light—something—to stop this.

Twenty minutes later, I'd calmed down. He hadn't come looking for me, but maybe he thought I'd just stepped out to go for a walk. And that's what I had done, after all. My restless energy had propelled me up a hill, the sick, hollow feeling ever-present. At least I no longer felt like I was going to lose my pasta when I saw him.

I just kept thinking, *Was it all just for show?* In the end, I couldn't forget I'd stayed in Germany after he got back to Kugelfels for him. Because he needed me to stay to make it all look real. It would've seemed strange if I'd taken off back to the States without him. But the time at the resort had felt so real. It was surreal at first, of course, but we hadn't been performing for anyone. He'd chosen to spend time with me. He'd chosen to kiss me and flirt with me.

The sick feeling returned at the thought that he'd used me, but I brushed it away. He wasn't the kind of man to do that. I knew him. Maybe not everything about him, but I did know he wouldn't have pretended to get close to me in this insane time after being captured by terrorists just to sleep with me. The crazy tried talking, but I refused to listen.

And realistically, those papers had been on their way long before any of this happened. The timing made sense. It wasn't far off from what we'd always planned for the divorce. The five-year mark, which hit right on my birthday this summer. So I couldn't look at those and think that now, after all this, he'd wanted to...

I exhaled, shutting my eyes against the darkening sky. *He'd wanted to... what?* Did I really believe the plan had changed? That he'd want something different? He'd said it himself—he hadn't been with anyone. He hadn't dated the entire time we'd been together. He was ready for the freedom he'd earned fair and square. He'd been deprived.

Add to that his love language—physical touch. *Ugh.* My stomach bottomed out and I felt ill. I couldn't stay in this mental state, though. I had to go back into that tiny apartment and spend the night in his company, then drive to the airport with him tomorrow. I couldn't let the hurt and sadness and deep disappointment shatter me. Not yet.

I smiled at no one, willing my brain to produce some endorphins or something to help shoo away the sensation I suspected could be classified as a cousin to what a broken heart might feel like. I put that squarely out of my mind and returned, all smiles and refreshed-from-my-walk energy.

As I approached his door, I reminded myself I had a life to return to, anyway. Why obsess about this when I had plans, obligations, and things to do?

"Oh, good. I was starting to get worried." His deep voice came from the couch where he flicked through channels on the TV. If he looked up, I didn't see, my focus on my feet and the path to my things.

"Yeah. I got restless. I'm worried I won't be able to sleep before the flight, so I figured I'd better move a bit." I rummaged in my bag, setting out my clothes for sleep, and then a small pile that I'd don tomorrow. I needed everything prepped so I didn't have to flail around at the crack of dawn.

He nodded and mumbled something that sounded like *good idea.*

"Yeah," I replied weakly, all determination deflating at his disinterest and distance.

"When do you start back to school?" he asked.

"Wednesday. It'll be good to get back to the routine, and I don't want to miss any more than I already have." I smiled, though he couldn't see me, and I could hear the false sound in the tone of my voice. Yes, the routine would help. It would have to, because I could already tell this return trip would leave me with more than jet lag to recover from.

"Yeah. I'm the same. I just want to get back to the routine."

Back to the routine. Back to how things were before. *Right.*

I nodded, though it was useless considering he still faced the TV, then excused myself to the shower. I promised myself I wouldn't cry while in there. At this rate, I could wait till I got home and could spend all of tomorrow night crying before I scraped myself together and returned to school on Wednesday. I'd have Tuesday to drown my sorrows, do laundry, and get groceries.

Time had both flown and crawled, and by nine, I gave up. We needed to talk. We had to, but it didn't feel like either one of us knew how or where to start. In the end, we'd been practicing *not* talking for more than four and a half years. We'd only begun communicating in the last two weeks. Not even a full two weeks, for that matter.

I sat on the side of the bed for a long time, staring at my chipped toenail polish and wondering what to say before I lay down. The next thing I knew, my alarm shook me from sleep and it was time to go.

CHAPTER THIRTY

Noah

We were an hour out from the Munich airport when I finally broke.

"So..."

Brilliant start, idiot.

She adjusted in her seat so her body angled toward mine. I gripped the steering wheel, wishing we were sitting anywhere else but in the car on the way to drop her at the airport.

"So?"

I cleared my throat, surprised by the nerves. I shouldn't have been considering they'd been my constant companion these last twenty-four hours. "Well, how are you gettin' home from the airport?"

"Sarah's dropping off my car this morning. She has the spare key. That way, I didn't have to pay for parking or ride with someone I don't know." She brushed her hair out of her face.

A pang of need to touch her struck me. Seeing her touch the waves, even in my peripheral vision, made my hands feel utterly empty. "Good. That's good."

She nodded, and I wanted to roll my eyes at how clumsy this conversation felt. My mind scrambled for something of value to say. "Uh, so, when do you start back at work?"

"Wednesday."

She didn't sound upset, just remote. Remarkable, considering I'd asked her the same question last night—brilliant moves. We'd had so many free-flowing conversations that this stilted, awkward way of speaking to each other drove me insane.

"I guess your kids will be glad to see you." What a genius I was. What a mind-blowing artist of small talk.

"Yes. And I'm excited to see them. I've—" She cut herself off and turned her head away.

I glanced at her, but she focused on looking out the passenger window. "You what?"

She sighed. "I've never been gone during the year like this, but I suppose that's obvious."

Cement hardened in my gut. "Yeah, I guess not. I'm sorry you had to."

"Don't apologize again, Noah. I'm glad I could be here for you." Her voice softened. "I'm glad I came."

"Me too," I said immediately, automatically. I couldn't fully express just how much it meant to me that she'd come. And stayed.

"Even though the circumstances were awful, and I wish you'd never been through everything, I'm thankful for the time we had. It was amazing to see the Alps and a little of

Germany, and even to meet your friends." She twisted her fingers together in her lap but kept her face forward and her gaze on the road ahead.

I wanted to catch her eye. Was any part of being with me qualified as amazing? Because for me, it was all her. All the healing and beauty of the last week had come from being with her. Yes, the mountains were a glorious setting, and the resort had been impressive. But if we'd been holed up in my crap barracks room, I suspected, in the end, I would've felt the same as long as I got a chance to know her.

My stomach cramped. I did know her. Not all of her, but a lot more than I had, and I didn't want to say goodbye. This couldn't be it.

"I can't tell you how—" I cleared my throat, surprised by how thick and tight it felt. "I can't tell you how much the time with you has meant to me."

I felt her hand on my thigh and glanced over to see her looking at me, her face full of emotion and her eyes shining. I laced our fingers together, thankful I wouldn't have to shift for a few minutes. The contact soothed and excited, paradoxically, and yet felt completely familiar to me now since her touch always had the same effect.

"Me too," she said.

We didn't talk after that but held hands the rest of the way. Even when I had to let go to drive, she kept her hand there, and just that brought fresh waves of love and frustration washing through me.

I parked the car in a small lot near her Departure terminal, my whole body buzzing with discontentment and the sharp feeling this was all wrong. All completely wrong.

"I hope you'll—

"Maybe we should—"

We smiled at each other, then I nodded to her, giving her the right of way in the conversation.

"I was going to say maybe we should, you know, stay in touch better this time? I hate the idea of going back to not even being friends."

She looked at me tentatively, like she didn't want to look fully in my face or something bad might happen.

I couldn't stop myself then, because I loved her, and arriving at this moment when she would get on a plane and fly thousands of miles away without anything decided between us meant I had failed. What the hell had I been doing the last forty-eight hours? Why hadn't I proposed to the woman, down on my knees, begging her to give me a chance to just... have a chance?

I pulled her close and held her to me. Her arms wrapped around my neck and she pressed closer, holding me as tightly as I did her. My God, this hurt. I'd never had a tearful goodbye before a deployment. Well, not with anyone but my mom, and she generally kept it together pretty well. I'd never really gotten it. Not until now. Not until this moment when what felt like my whole world was ready to roll her busted suitcase into the airport and fly away.

"Yes, please. Let's text. Let's call. Let's do whatever you want. I'm not sure what I'm going to do with myself now that you're leavin'. I don't have any idea how to go back to normal life. I don't want to go back to what we were doin' before. Not at all." I pulled back and searched her eyes.

She swiped under her lower lids, brushing away tears, then glanced at her watch. "Okay. Good."

Out of time. We were finally out of time and I'd done nothing. I'd made no progress. I'd missed the hundred chances I should've taken, and the clawing inside my lungs reinforced the error.

"So you'll text me from the plane. And then you'll text me from Atlanta. And then you'll text me when you get home safe to your apartment." I was issuing commands but I couldn't help it. I wanted her to understand that I wanted *everything* from her. Not just important updates. Not just the highlights. I wanted the minute details. I should've said it all sooner.

"Okay," she said, a little laugh tumbling out with a half-smile.

I crushed her to me again, shutting my eyes against the absolute sledgehammer of pain and longing and love and sadness beating against my chest from the inside out. *I love you. I love you. Please stay.*

But I wouldn't say it. Not until I could trust I meant it and that she wanted it. I wouldn't say anything she might respond to out of that lingering sense of debt she seemed to carry, however foolish the notion was.

After a few moments, she pulled back. "Okay, I've got to go. If I stand here much longer, I won't be able to leave."

She leaned in and pressed her lips to mine, a firm, rushed, agonizing kiss. Then she reached for the handle of her suitcase, hitched her carry-on onto her shoulder, and took a deep breath. "I'll miss you, Noah."

I needed water. My throat had been coated in petrified tree bark that kept me from swallowing. My jaw ached when I scratched out, "Me too, baby. Text me from the plane."

CHAPTER THIRTY-ONE

Katie

I stared at twenty-two smiling faces, most of which were moving—jumping, clapping, waving. "Mrs. Miller!" They swarmed me, hugging my legs, and pulling at my hands. And I felt the horrible belt of stress and sadness and missing Noah loosen a notch.

The first day back had flown by. Getting up to speed again and calming the kids' overexcitement proved exhausting, especially since by the time the school day ended, my body thought it was bedtime. When I returned to my apartment, I pulled out my phone to message Noah and saw he'd beat me to it.

"I hope your first day back went well. I bet the kids were so excited to see you. I'm jealous of a bunch of six-year-olds."

I chuckled, but my heart twisted in pleasure and pain. I'd left Germany confused and sad, and if I forced myself to be honest, even the tiniest bit hopeful. I didn't know what to expect when he dropped me off, and as horrible as saying goodbye felt, I'd found some small sense of relief in seeing his distress. He hadn't been stoic or even quiet. He'd hugged me, and I could've sworn desperation drove his words and the way he'd clutched me to him.

He'd responded to every text I'd sent on the way back. When I'd switched over to my regular phone, I'd almost felt sad to be rid of the little burner phone. But now I could keep a record of our conversation more easily. He'd messaged me throughout the day yesterday, and I'd texted back. We'd kept up a stream of conversation, and seeing that he hadn't disappeared yet gave me another little dash of hope.

We hadn't discussed the divorce papers. We hadn't really discussed anything, and a big part of me felt pretty angry about that. But I had to direct that anger at myself, too. I'd had chances to bring it all up, and I'd blazed past them, clutching at my pride and fear and desire not to upset things too much before we parted.

His mom had texted me every few days of the trip and I always responded. She wanted my perspective on how he was doing. She didn't press or pry about anything else. But when I got her message when I touched down in North Carolina, all I could do was give her a thumbs up in response to her, "*I hope you readjust well and school finishes smoothly. I'd love to talk soon.*"

I'd see my therapist tomorrow, and that was overdue. I needed to talk through things with her. It'd all been such an insane whirlwind, and I never would've guessed I'd be stumbling back to the States about two weeks later feeling happy and desolate and so full of love I could burst.

"*I think the energy expended by my kids today could've powered the next Mars rover.*"

Immediately, a little bubble popped up showing he was responding. My heart leaped, but I forced myself to put the phone down and make dinner instead of staring at the screen and waiting for his words.

"Are you feeling okay? Jet lag getting to you?"

He'd always been considerate and sweet. But now that I knew him, taking things like this to be purely a kind gesture instead of some kind of sign that he loved me and wanted me too had become insanely difficult. I messaged back.

"Definitely sleepy, but doing okay. Shouldn't you be heading to bed?"

We chatted back and forth for a while, talking about our days, and then he asked if we could talk—actually talk—this weekend. I agreed, my heart thumping in my chest as I sent the response. I knew what this would be. He'd tell me to expect the papers in the mail. He'd be ready to push things forward, and I'd have to keep it together. I'd need to make sure we just did a regular phone call, no video.

I went to bed by eight, the exhaustion and sadness and sense of inevitable *endings* consuming me and cutting through any joy or expectation that had come from our exchange.

"So, how was your week back at work?" Did my voice sound higher?

"Not bad. It actually felt pretty good. We're preppin' for a new rotation in a few days. I've checked in with Dr. Wagner every few days even though I have a new guy here —I like him. And have only had one more nightmare."

I curled my knees to my chest and cradled the phone

against my cheek while we talked. "That's good. I'm so glad."

I wished I could've been there for him, even for just that one.

He stayed quiet a moment, and the nerves that'd followed me around since I'd woken at six this morning jumped in response to his silence.

"What about you?" His voice sounded low and somber.

"Me? It went well. The kids readjusted to me quickly, and I'm back in the routine. You know, same old, same old." I infused my voice with cheeriness, mostly because my anxious mind apparently wouldn't let me sound normal.

"Good. But I meant, how's it goin' with the nightmares for you?"

I sat up a bit, surprised. "Oh. Well, they aren't really an issue for me most of the time. I'd say I have one every few months, max. And it's usually related to something I talk about in therapy. But thankfully, it's not something I think about every day anymore, and I think that helps."

"That's good. I'm still sorry I made you talk about it last week." Concern laced through his words.

Last week. Had it only been last week? It felt like both minutes and years ago we were together at the beautiful Austrian resort, just the two of us getting to know each other and falling in love.

Well, one of us, anyway.

"Please don't apologize. I'm glad we talked through it. And you helped with the bad dream, too." My stomach flipped at the memory of him holding me the rest of the night. In many ways, it'd been that contact, those quiet moments nested together, that'd set us on this course. Again, me, anyway.

"It wasn't exactly a hardship." His voice emerged a little rough.

"No?"

"No."

Oh. Well, that was good news, at least.

Annoyingly, being apart from him meant I questioned everything about our relationship. I cursed my insecurity. We hadn't talked and clarified anything, but when I left, I felt sure he cared for me in some ways, that he wanted me in some ways, too. But the longer we were apart, the less certain of anything I felt.

He cleared his throat, and I wished I could see him. I wondered if he was sitting or standing. If he was wearing jeans or comfy clothes. Was he on the couch in his apartment? Was he wandering around outside?

"So, listen. I need to talk to you about somethin', and I want you to feel free to tell me how you feel. I need you to promise me you won't say what you think I want to hear or what you think you *should say*. Not that I think you do that, but we're not in person, so I can't read you."

I could hear rustling in the background like he'd put his hands to work during the conversation. I focused on that instead of the dropping sensation in my belly, and the way I couldn't quite take a full breath.

"I'll do my best," I said, hoping I didn't sound as terrified and upset as I felt.

"Good. Thank you." Then, nothing until I heard him swear under his breath.

"What's going on, Noah?"

A gusty exhale came across the line, each sound sending my heart higher into my throat.

"I should've done this in person."

My stomach clenched and I eked out a shaky, "Okay."

A quick huff sounded then. "I got the divorce papers from my lawyer in the mail the day we came back."

My throat dried out, but my heart rate slowed and I forced a slow exhale. "I saw them."

"You did?"

"Yes. I should've said something too, but things already seemed strained."

"I know. It was on me and I should've brought it up. It's no one's fault, really. We had a whirlwind time together, to put it mildly, so ending it all talking about a divorce seemed cruel."

My jaw pinched and my heart throbbed with an ache I'd felt a low-level version of all week since we'd said good-bye. But now, as we faced a true and lasting farewell, it pulsed and pulsed and pulsed with the injury.

Then mercifully, a knock came at my door and the door-bell rang. Sarah was early for our brunch date.

"Uh, sorry, someone's at my door." I pulled open the door but pressed a finger to my lips. Sarah frowned at me but entered my apartment.

"Oh, should we talk another time, then?" His voice sounded frustrated.

"Probably, yeah." I tried to sound regretful, but I could only think about escaping this conversation. I knew it was stupid and entirely futile, but if we didn't both agree, if he didn't send the papers, then maybe I'd be able to keep him a bit longer.

I could hide from this. For just a little while longer, I could hide and delay, and it wouldn't be over just yet.

"Just let me know when."

I agreed, and then he hung up, and Sarah knew by the look on my face I needed her, so she wrapped her arms around me and let me cry.

CHAPTER THIRTY-TWO

Noah

I heard nothing from her for two days, then got a text that asked about my day. She was hiding.

The rotation started in eighteen hours, and we wouldn't talk then. In reality, there was no urgency. No looming deadline, though it felt like there was. My mind had convinced me that if I didn't know how she felt about me—about us—then I'd lose it.

But in truth, we had time, and I'd have to take it. I'd tricked myself into believing we had time when she visited, but we didn't. I'd used up the little we had with playing a game of chicken with myself, and in the end, I won and lost. I didn't put myself out on the line, but I didn't get what I wanted, either.

Now, all we had was time, assuming she didn't demand a divorce. She clearly didn't want to have the conversation about the papers, which I took to be a possible good sign.

Maybe it meant she didn't like the idea anymore, though it might also mean she just didn't want to end something that'd been a part of both our lives for so long. Even if she looked forward to life after being Mrs. Miller, that didn't mean it would be easy to just move on.

But the days without her, now the *nine* days without her, had plodded on unbearably. And clarity sharpened my focus even as it slapped me across the face for being an idiot. Why hadn't I just confessed my feelings, at least to some small degree, before she left? I'd begged her to stay in touch, true, but I could've said I wanted to date her. I could've said I wanted to be together, even if apart.

I could've said I love you. Don't leave me. Never leave me.

But not so much. She had a life and plans, and I didn't know how to reconcile that reality with what I wanted. But I knew I couldn't wait around forever. I couldn't let the distance fester between us and become something that blocked our ability—our very newly learned ability, mind you—to communicate.

I'd grappled with whether my feelings were real. A huge component of my ridiculous fear of confessing my love for her came from the fear that the time in Afghanistan had messed me up. That it'd created a false sense of intimacy rather than pushing us together for a chance to create a real one. And though Dr. Wagner refused to just tell me what to do, damn him, the distance between me and Katie hadn't changed my feelings. At least, it hadn't diminished them.

I'd debated what to say to her beyond the surface level nonsense of the past few minutes. But I had a few errands to run before all the offices closed for the day—if I didn't get it done today, I'd be out of luck for the next two weeks while we were on rotation.

I landed on something straightforward. *"I'd like to talk again soon, but I'm going to be working non-stop for the next two weeks. Please tell me we can talk after that."*

I hit the mailroom and got gas before I heard back, but relief flooded when I saw her response. *"Of course. I'm sorry we got interrupted on Saturday. Stay safe at work."*

"I will. You too. I'll miss talking to you." I had to toss in something to hint. Because maybe she believed, a bit like I felt, we'd reverted to how things were before. Granted, we'd never texted like this, never kept in touch so regularly. But we weren't doing much beyond cordial check-ins.

"I'll miss talking to you, too. You won't have your phone?"

"I will, but service is iffy in the box. Feel free to text me, and I'll respond whenever I can."

With that, I shut the door and made my way to the Education Center, where a sign on the door said *Now Hiring!* Good to know.

I stepped into an unusually busy lobby and surprisingly saw several familiar faces standing in a small semicircle.

"Miller! Are you coming to the briefing, too?" Thatcher Wild greeted me with his typical friendly smile and enthusiasm.

"Briefing?" I shuffled through my mental schedule but nothing clicked.

Rob Waverly spoke from my left. "The EMU is here to recruit officers and a few NCOs."

Our eyes met with shared understanding.

We'd talked a bit after Katie left. He'd been back at Kugelfels and rehabbing his hand, so he couldn't take extended leave just yet. He'd taken a long weekend and said he was doing okay mentally. I felt the same. So far, anyway. But he'd seemed restless in a way I definitely didn't feel unless I thought about Katie. She made me want things and dream of things. But Rob was looking for something and didn't have a woman in mind.

His being here made sense then. We'd been rescued by Exceptional Mission Unit operatives, and they were the best. Literally, they were the best and most elite military war-fighting unit in the world. Who *wouldn't* want to learn what it took to join their ranks?

Roscoe Sherman, a specialist from my platoon, broke through that thought. "Miller, you gotta tell us what happened. Cap'n Waverly won't give us anything. It was EMU that got you guys, right?"

I shook my head once. "Sorry, man, I don't remember a thing."

Sherman looked peeved. "Yeah, that's what he said, too."

I shrugged, then gave Rob a slight nod but spoke to him, Wild, and three others who stood waiting for the briefing. "Well, this sounds interesting. I've got a meeting with one of the counselors, so you'll have to give me the info later."

"Will do," Wild responded.

I stepped away, relieved Sherman hadn't pressed. I guessed if it came to it, I could always just have said, "Sorry, I signed a confidentiality agreement," but that struck me as less than ideal.

Then two things happened at once. Wild's eyes caught on something over my shoulder, and he did a double-take, his mouth falling open just when I heard a voice say, "Sergeant Miller?"

"That's me. Good luck," I said, eyeing Wild one last time before turning to find a woman with dark hair waiting for me.

"Are you Sergeant Miller? We're strangely busy today."

She smiled and gestured toward an office with a door standing wide open.

"Yeah, most of that group up front is waiting for the EMU brief." I settled into the seat across from her desk.

She spoke from behind me. "Oh, that's right. The guys here to present seemed nice. I'd never suspect they were super soldiers. I—"

I twisted in my seat to see what'd caused her to break off and saw her with the door closed about seventy percent of the way. She was staring at Thatcher Wild, and he was staring right back through the small opening.

Wild raised a hand, and a sharp inhale came from the woman, but she raised her hand too, then after a beat, she shut the door. I turned back quickly, flipping open the planner and notebook I'd brought.

She sat, more like slumped, into her seat and steadied herself with two hands on the desk in front of her. When she raised one to push some hair behind her ear, her fingers shook.

"Are you all right?" I couldn't help but ask.

She blinked, evidently startled to find me sitting in front of her.

"Oh, uh, yes. Of course. Sorry." She rose to her feet and her hand shot out. "Bec Jones."

I stood and shook it, then we both sat.

"So, how can I help you today?"

When I opened Ms. Jones's office door, Wild stepped in front of me.

"Sorry, Miller. Didn't mean to—"

He looked winded and worn out, his usual energy and

kindness eclipsed by whatever had passed between him and the counselor.

"You okay, man?" I asked, surveying him for bodily injuries.

"Yeah, good. Just need to talk to Bec—Ms. Jones." His voice, like the rest of him, spoke to the unusual situation.

"Uh, I think the Ed Center closes pretty much now, but—"

"I'm going in. Catch you later." He cut me off and stepped inside, shutting the door behind him.

I wouldn't have thought Thatcher could look like that. I mean, I'd seen the guy stressed out, exhausted, even angry, but that run-over-by-a-tank expression? I wished I knew the story there.

I tucked my items under my arm and made my way to the car, but I stopped a few feet from it when I saw Waverly and a small group talking to a man I immediately recognized. Seemed stupid to know someone just by their face when I'd seen said face for a matter of minutes, if not seconds, and then promptly passed out. But there he stood in khaki pants and a button-down plaid shirt, nice brown leather shoes, and hair longer than anyone else's in the group that surrounded him.

He must've felt my stare because he glanced in my direction. His eyes narrowed almost imperceptibly, and he nodded in that same barely there way. I nodded back, my head feeling big and clumsy, but his attention had already returned to the group. I dropped into my car, shut the door, and chugged water from the bottle I always kept with me, my throat unbearably dry.

I'd never imagined seeing him again—the man who'd rescued me. I'd never seen any of his team's faces. A nod, a moment of mutual understanding—it wasn't enough. It didn't even begin to address the gratitude and wretchedness that welled in me at the sight of him, at knowing he'd risked himself, his team, to get me and Waverly out.

As I sat there, too worked up to drive, I let my heart pound out its drama, breathing through the odd rush of adrenaline the memories and feelings stirred. And in me grew something like resolve.

I'd made it out of an impossible situation. That soldier, badass EMU operator though he may be, was just a man. And he and his team had risked their lives to get me out. How could I possibly live the rest of my life without going hard after what I wanted? Didn't I owe it to them to live a full life? And more so, didn't I owe it to myself?

That night, I called my mom.

"I'm pretty sure I messed up. Bad. Worse than I even realized." Because why hadn't I just grown a pair and laid it all out?

"I don't think it's beyond repair."

I shut my eyes, praying with everything in me she was right. "I hope not. But I don't know what to do or how to fix everything. Or even how to start over. Again."

And then my mom confirmed what I'd been barreling toward for hours, or really weeks, but possibly years. "Noah, don't you lose her. Do what it takes, whatever that might be, and make sure she understands that you want a real life with her."

A real life with her.

Yes. Exactly.

CHAPTER THIRTY-THREE

Katie

I didn't expect to hear from Noah, but I'd decided I wanted to text him. He seemed like, maybe, he might want to hear from me. The *I'll miss talking to you* was something small, maybe, but I latched onto it with all my strength.

So I messaged him. Just small things—stories about my day, asking how he was doing, or sometimes little memories from the time we'd shared together. Those made my blood rush in my ears after I sent them, like he'd somehow sense the emotions behind them.

I didn't get a response for the first three days, but on Friday, his text came through. At first, he'd just responded to the texts I'd sent. But then, he'd sent new ones, more in the vein of the memories of our time together.

"Remember the kaiserschmarm? Sometimes I daydream about that vanilla sauce."

"I'll never forget your face when you came back from the spa that first time. I can't believe I forgot to tell you everyone would be naked."

"I wish we were sledding on a glacier right now."

To that, I'd responded, *"Me too. That was such a great day."*

And he'd sent back, *"All of it?"*

And with a breathlessness that made no sense considering he was nowhere in sight and couldn't see me, I responded, *"Yes, every minute."* I'd relived that first kiss more than once, and thinking of it now made me ache for him.

All the memories had the power to send my pulse racing, and I realized something was happening. We weren't just volleying greetings and recaps of our days. We were flirting. Having fun.

Granted, via text, but we didn't have any other option right now. And suddenly, I stopped dreading the phone call that would come at the end of his rotation. I started looking forward to it, unable to wait to hear what he'd say, because I knew—*I knew*—somewhere soul-deep, he wouldn't be messaging with me this way if he meant to end it all with those papers.

By the end of his two weeks, my heart, if it hadn't already been full of love and hope for him, would've been overflowing. But I'd left Germany with a heart bursting, though troubled and fearful. Those feelings weren't gone, either, but I no longer felt the need to avoid talking to him. To hide from what he might say about those papers. I felt embarrassed remembering how juvenile I'd been in ghosting him for days.

I'd dissected it from every angle in my own mind, with Sarah and with Maria, my therapist. My tendency toward insecurity had me floundering, feeling like I couldn't trust the things I thought I knew about our relationship. And that first stretch after I'd left, maybe I couldn't or shouldn't have.

But one night over dinner, when I'd told Sarah I thought it had happened too fast, that maybe it was just the weird glamour of the experience, she'd made her opinion clear.

"Remind me how long you guys have been married?" She dipped a chip into a large bowl of bright green guacamole.

"A few weeks shy of five years." I studied her, wondering where she'd take this.

"And how long have you known him?"

"About seven."

"And how long have you had a crush on him?" Her dark blond brow arched over one eye.

My cheeks flamed, but I answered. "Probably about seven, but definitely for five with varying degrees of intensity."

She nodded. "And when you were in Germany, you essentially had breakfast, lunch, and dinner together, plus that magical snack time. Plus, you spent every day together doing stuff, right?"

I chuckled at her saying *magical snack time*, but only because it very aptly described how I felt about the meal. "Yes."

She squinted and studied the ceiling a moment, then snapped. "By my count, that's essentially equivalent to somewhere around thirty dates, and that's being conservative. That's not including the time in the hospital, or the weird Army marriage retreat thing."

"Thirty? No way. I was in Germany for just under two weeks."

"Sure, but in that time, you packed in a lot of mileage. You nursed him back to health, you—"

"I didn't *nurse* him in any way. He was in the hospital."

She held up a hand. "You helped him recover and saw him at a really low point. You talked through some of your hard stuff and some of his. You traveled together, experienced new things together, shared a gorgeous luxury resort that I'm totally jealous of together. And you talked a ton, from what you've said. Not to mention the physical connection you seem to have." She wiggled her eyebrows at me.

I inhaled slowly, the flush of heat at my cheeks once again, and a sudden fizzing feeling in my chest. "It felt like we shared a whole lot in a short amount of time."

She took my hand and smiled kindly. "That's because you did, and even though you haven't been close for that long, it doesn't surprise me something developed between you. Not just because you had this crazy experience, but also because you've always cared for him. And I'd bet he's always cared for you."

I'd left that lunch feeling less foolish and lovesick, and more hopeful and determined. I wished I hadn't been so full of doubt—of myself, and him, and the way forward—while we were together in person. But I couldn't go back to that, so when we'd talk next, I'd be honest, no matter how nerve-racking or how antsy it might make me.

And now, I'd had my punishment, and the brutal wait between messages had taught me the lesson I should've already learned. In truth, I already had. I didn't want to be apart from Noah in any sense, and avoiding him created distance I couldn't stand.

But two days after I expected to hear from him, I'd only gotten spare texts. Nothing good or meaningful. And more than that, they were still sporadic just like they'd been during the rotation. He'd already told me when it had ended—more than forty-eight hours ago. Which made my stomach sour and my hopes shrivel, though I tried to resist it.

I pushed against the thoughts telling me I'd ruined everything, and I'd lost my chance. Though I'd managed them, I'd wrestled with the fear, doubt, and sense that maybe I *had* missed my chance. I rejected all of that, reminding myself that self-doubt had no place here. If I'd misunderstood, then so be it. If he didn't feel the same, I couldn't change that. If we landed on the same page with our feelings, but couldn't figure out a way to make it work and be together, I couldn't control that. But I could give myself the gift of being honest with him, and then I could move forward without regret.

I drove home from my weekly grocery run full of wishes. On the way, I let little daydreams pop into my head, thinking of Noah and remembering his touch, his eyes, the way he'd grab my hand or tuck my hair behind my ear.

I parked my car outside my apartment building and saw a tall blond guy loitering in front of the building. A man who looked a whole lot like Noah. My breath rushed out of me as I hustled across the street, a weird, strangled *"Noah?"* issuing from my throat when I got close.

He turned and a smile flashed across his face before he held out his arms to me. Instinctively, I moved to him, wrapping my arms around him in a rush of relief and longing and more than a little confusion.

"What are you doing here?" My voice emerged high and strained with disbelief.

"We have things to talk about, and they deserve to be said face to face. *We* deserve it. I should've talked with you before you left, but I wussed out, so... here I am." He spoke into my hair because we held each other tightly.

I pulled back to survey him. He looked good. So, so good. My stomach fluttered. I stepped back and brought my hands with me, though they wanted to stay attached to the man in front of me. He was here! Right here with me, and I wanted to celebrate and kiss him and pull him inside and never let him leave.

Hope and worry warred in me. He couldn't have come all this way just to bring me those divorce papers. It just didn't make sense.

"Can we maybe go inside?" he asked, stuffing his hands in his pockets.

That's when I fully registered he stood there on my street, a small duffel bag at his feet. He'd been waiting for me, and I'd been gone for hours this morning. What if he'd been standing right here since I left?

"Of course. Follow me. How long have you been here?" I led the way through my building, anticipation and curiosity swirling in my chest and compressing my lungs. I hadn't caught my breath since I'd seen him outside.

"Just an hour or so. I caught a red-eye, but it took me a minute to get a ride over. And then I went to that café a couple blocks away once I realized you weren't here." His footfalls were heavy in the hallway.

"You must be tired." I glanced at him, unlocking the door, and my stomach flipped when I caught his eyes sliding over me, unmistakable appreciation in his gaze.

His attention flicked up to my face. "Definitely tired but very glad to be here."

The heat in his eyes stole what remained of my breath. He'd always been arrestingly handsome, and that'd only increased after the time we'd shared. Add to that the time apart, and I didn't know how to handle this man looking at me like that.

"I'm glad you're here, too."

We walked into the apartment, and I found myself immensely glad I'd done a deep clean the day before, and curious if he planned to drop his duffel and stay. With me. Here.

Because that had to mean something. All of this did. But I wasn't about to be the one to get the discussion started, whatever it might be, when he'd just flown across the Atlantic to do so.

"All right, before I wuss out again, I've got to talk to you." His brow pulled low, and he crossed his arms and widened his stance like he needed to brace for the conversation.

"Please, go ahead." I gestured in front of me like *the floor is yours* and sat lightly on the edge of the couch arm.

He shifted on his feet, settling into that broad position and tucking his hands into his pockets.

"At the retreat, I got confused. I was havin' a lot of feelings." His eyes flickered up to mine, then back to the spot on the coffee table where he'd focused when he spoke. "When I spoke to Dr. Wagner, he said somethin' he'd said a few times before, but in that moment, it really hit me. The gist of it was that makin' big changes or huge decisions right after a traumatic experience is ill-advised. We don't always know how we're going to feel when the highs and lows of that experience level out, so changin' things fundamental to our lives—jobs, relationships, location, etc.—is a bad idea."

I listened, watched, and waited. Every molecule of my attention focused on him and his words. I didn't have a response to that other than to nod, which he took as a sign to continue.

"I'd been thinkin' of suggesting we consider delaying the divorce."

His blue eyes hit me when he said those words, and the force of them would've leveled a city street if I hadn't absorbed the impact. I felt it physically—that look, those words—and rocked back from the blow.

He nodded, as though to say *yeah* and continued. "I felt like we had a real connection, and everything I learned about you, I liked. Everything we did together—out in the world and just the two of us—added up to be some of the best moments of my life. My *life*."

My breath came shallow, his words stirring in me a frantic feeling. I needed him to make sense of all this. He couldn't be saying these things just to get to the end and declare he wanted to separate.

He took a few steps in my direction, then stopped himself. "I'd been thinkin' I wanted to explore the future with you. Right up until that lunch where you talked about your work and grad program, and then the phone call when I realized maybe all my thoughts and feelings weren't trustworthy."

The quiet in my apartment felt thick. I wished the AC unit would kick on to give us background noise because, otherwise, there was a huge likelihood he could hear my heart trying to pound out of my chest.

"*Not trustworthy.*" I echoed the words, my voice hollow.

"It's why I withdrew there at the end of your trip. That, and again, hearin' you talk about how much you loved your job, and hearin' you talk about the master's program and what a big deal it is." He took another step closer, hands still in his pockets.

Since my apartment wasn't huge, he now stood just two feet away. I wanted to reach out and grab his hands, connect him to me now that he finally existed in the same room. But he seemed to need to stand apart while he spoke, and I still didn't know where he planned to go with all this.

"Why does me loving my job or my master's program have anything to do with this?" I crossed my arms, feeling exposed and incredibly unsure, even as my heart banged around in my chest.

He inched closer.

Standing straight and strong, he didn't look away when he spoke. "I'd been thinkin' about a real life together, which would involve living together. I owe the Army time, and I also plan for it to be my career. So that would mean you bein' with me and movin' away from the school and your master's program."

Butterflies fluttered by the thousands in my chest. *A real life together.* My heart and mind held hands and screamed *Yes!* in unison, but I pressed my lips closed so I wouldn't say something crazy. Because he still spoke like none of it would actually work out.

When I didn't speak, he continued.

"I realized I couldn't ask you to give that up. You've worked so hard to get where you are. That was the point of our marriage to begin with, so how could I then ask you to throw it all away and be with me?"

I stood, arms still crossed over my chest. "The point, in the beginning, was to get me away from my stepfather and stepbrother so they had no way to hurt me."

"Yes, and give you resources. And before I sound like a saint, give me extra money from bein' married and gettin' BAH." One eyebrow arched in sardonic challenge.

I rolled my eyes. "I think we both know I got the better end of the deal there."

He shook his head and stepped closer again.

"No, I did. Because without that *deal*, you never would've been there with me at Landstuhl. And you never would've given me the best week of my life." Color rose to his cheeks.

My whole face warmed when I agreed. "It was mine, too."

He swallowed, his Adam's apple bobbing like maybe doing so proved difficult. "The point is, I started doubting. And then when I talked to my therapist, I had this horrible thought that I was tryin' to force something that wasn't even there."

My eyes fluttered, absorbing this news. How could he ever think this between us was all in his head?

Except, hadn't I done something similar when we were parting? Didn't I talk myself into believing it was for the best?

It was time to woman up and tell this man—who'd traveled across the world for me—the truth. "It was there. I felt it. I *feel* it."

"Me too. Maybe it makes me insane or stupid, but I love you, Katie. I'm in love with you, and I don't want us to divorce. I don't want us to be apart."

As he spoke, he moved, and so did I. By the end, he was speaking the words right to my lips before he pressed against me, and finally, after weeks that felt like months, we kissed.

Relief and thrill and joy, and a thick line of uncertainty, swirled within me as his mouth devoured mine for delectable minutes. He pulled back and looked happy, though his brow still furrowed.

"I'll admit, I don't know how to do it logistically. I can feasibly cut my tour in Germany short if they'll let me. And I can try to get stationed at Bragg, again, if they'll let me.

But that'll take time, and I want us to have time together sooner than that. We're still learnin' about each other, and I want to be able to do that without an ocean between us."

I laughed, the pure delight at his words, at finally knowing how he felt, lightening my limbs and making me feel like I could float. "I'd love that. I love you, and I want the same for us."

His blue eyes flashed, and then he bent to kiss me again, this time with less relief and more unbridled desire. He released me, his chest rising and falling just like mine.

"I'm sorry I didn't say this before you left. I'm so sorry." He brushed his nose along mine in a sweet, comforting gesture.

"I should've said something, too. I should've asked you about the papers instead of getting upset and clamming up. You've done so much for me, and I didn't want you to feel you owed me something for being there. I never wanted you to feel I was a burden."

His hands cupped my cheeks, and he spoke low and almost severely. "You owe me nothing. I've been in awe of you these last few years, and I couldn't be happier to know you love me. It's the best news I've ever heard. Please tell me that none of this has to do with you feelin' you owe me."

I shook my head in his hands. "I don't. I mean, I often have felt that way, and I can't pretend I haven't. But I don't love you because I owe it to you, Noah. Is part of the reason I love you because of what you've done for me? Yes. It has to be. But it's not because of the thing in itself. It's because it points to who you are—someone honorable and thoughtful and so kind it's ridiculous."

He sighed. "Katie, you know what I've gotten out of this."

"Yes, but you've been starved. At the retreat, when you

said your love preference was physical touch, I felt sick. All these years, you've kept yourself from relationships—which I'm completely happy about, not to confuse the issue—but I realized how you must've been just aching for affection and connection. I hate that you've not only been alone, but unable to have that expression of love." I stroked down his arms, endeavoring to replenish some of what he'd missed out on.

He crowded me, pressing against me. "I've been lonely, just like you. I haven't had anyone to touch me or anyone to touch back, but that only means one thing."

My belly dropped, the texture in his voice and his words causing heat to coil low. "What does it mean?"

He grinned. "It means we have a lot to make up for."

CHAPTER THIRTY-FOUR

Noah

We lay in her bed, her head on my chest, and her hair blanketing my skin. Her fingers traced idly across my collarbone, her eyes following the movement but clearly lost in thought. I'd never felt more at peace than in this moment. Nothing had been decided, but she loved me. That changed everything. It meant everything.

"What are you thinkin' about?" I asked, my voice just more than a whisper.

Without lifting her head, her eyes shifted to me. "Wondering if Kugelfels elementary is hiring."

The small curve at the corners of her mouth paired with that statement had me sitting up and sliding back to rest against the headboard. She rose and sat on her knees as she faced me, a sheet tucked tightly, and unfortunately, around her.

"You want to move to Kugelfels?" I took her hand in

mine, entirely uninterested in living without her touch while here.

"Yes. If I can."

"You can. Of course you can. I mean, it'll take a minute to get you command sponsorship and figure out the housing situation. I'm not sure how that works, but I'm sure Colonel Wolfe will do whatever he can to help us work it out." With my free hand, I pulled a length of her hair through my fingers.

"It won't cause problems?"

There she went, being the sweetest woman on earth. "No, baby. It'll be great. Though I have to tell you, I'm more concerned about your master's program."

She exhaled long and slow. "I've been thinking about that a lot. I don't want to have to give up on that dream entirely, but I have options. I can talk to them about deferring, and if they won't allow it, I can always reapply when we come back stateside."

That *we* had me feeling ten feet tall, like Maximus in the stadium after defeating a hundred men. We sounded right after the time apart had only been wrong.

I hadn't spoken, so she continued.

"Maybe it makes me weak or silly to put that off for you, but I don't see it that way. I see our being together as investing in the future in a way that has a much longer reach than even continuing my education. And I'm not giving that up, nor will I. I know it'll be much more difficult if we're together. But what's the point if I'm miserable without you and can't enjoy and learn like I'd planned?"

Her voice had gained a defensive edge, and I smoothed a hand down her arm. "I'm certainly not going to dissuade you, as long as you promise we'll keep talkin' about it. I would never call you weak or silly you're neither of those things nor have you ever been. And if we need to jockey to get back to Bragg so you can be in the same program, we will. There are no guarantees, but I think it'd be doable eventually."

She nodded. "We'll see what the university says first and go from there."

"Sounds reasonable enough to me. I should say it's pretty difficult to find a teaching job, though. There's a huge pool of teachers and not enough jobs. Livie may know something about it."

"I figured it could be tricky. Not ideal, but if I can't teach, maybe there's something else. Or maybe I can do some of my grad program online." She fiddled with my fingers, threading and unthreading them where we held hands.

"I saw that the Education Center is hiring. Or, they were before rotation. Who knows if they filled the position already? But that'd be in education, at least. Not elementary, obviously, and not administration exactly. But it could be somethin' if the school doesn't work out. And you know, you don't have to work."

I'll take care of you. Always. I stopped short of that, not wanting to seem overbearing, though I wanted to take care of her any way she'd let me.

She gave me a soft smile. "Thank you for saying that, but I want to work. What would I do all day while you're at work? I'll need a way to meet people and make friends, and build a life there."

"You're really considering it." My heart thudded as I said it, the reality of her genuinely wanting to be with me finally sinking in.

Her head tilted to one side. "Should I not be?"

"Yes. I mean, *no*, you should be."

She moved closer, and I rested a hand on her waist while she brought her palm gently to my face. "I am. I've got a lot to deal with here—getting out of my lease and storing my stuff and dealing with the school."

A glimmer of doubt flashed across her face.

"What?"

"I guess all of that depends on you truly wanting me there. I'm not doubting you, but this would be a huge change to both our lives. You're used to being single, and I'm used to just doing my own thing." She bit her lip as she waited for my reply.

I surged up, drawing our faces close and kissing her, claiming that bottom lip for my own. After a few moments, we parted, and I reminded her of something essential.

"I wasn't single. I was married, living overseas. I wasn't out on the town. I rarely went out with people. I did travel, but mostly alone, and not that much, either. I work a lot and volunteer when someone needs help. I work out a lot. I cook a lot. I read a lot and watch movies and play video games. These are all things you would supersede, or could join me for if you wanted."

She chuckled. "Okay. I believe you. But I do think it's going to take some time to adjust, especially if we're living together."

"If? You can't move to Germany and not live with me if you're—"

Her hand on my mouth, just a touch to my lips, quieted me. "I don't mean it like that. I just mean it's a huge change. Our relationship is only a month old, and that's being generous. It's kind of an insane thing to do."

"I hear you. I'm sure you're right. But I think it's different that we've known each other a long time and have been linked in a significant way for years. We may not have behaved like married people in any sense in those years, but it's not like we just met."

Her clear brown eyes blinked back at me, and the smile that came with my words made me feel like my heart doubled in size.

"No, we haven't just met. And we have a history together, even though it's nothing like what a real relationship would be like."

I held up both hands, displaying innocence. "I'll just say I tried to get you to give me more updates, and let me know how you were. You were stingy with your information."

She opened her mouth in shock. "What? *I* was stingy? Whenever you were in town, you'd hardly talk to me! I'd suggest we meet for lunch before whatever errands we had to do, and you'd always give excuses."

I lowered my arms and reached to wrap them around her. Then I rolled us so she lay on her back, and I propped up on one hand, leaning over her so our faces were inches apart. "I always knew if I let you in even a little, if I gave you just an inch, you'd take a mile. Since we'd planned to divorce, it was an odd, mostly unconscious kind of self-preservation."

Her gaze was hot, and just returning it made my heart pound.

"I guess you were right."

"Guess I was."

I hadn't seen Katie in over six weeks. *Six. Weeks.*

We'd spent an amazing weekend together, but I'd only had four days of leave, and that had been pushing it, so I couldn't extend my trip. She'd had to stay in Raleigh and prepare to move, and though it would've been amazing to have her jump on a plane the day I flew back, she still had to wrap things up with the school and pack up her apartment. Her lease was set to renew the following month, so it made sense for her not to rush. Add to that, she couldn't really stay in my bachelor quarters, and it made sense.

It did. But it was categorically the worst.

We'd talked every day. Sometimes, it was just messages, and a few times, we'd missed each other due to bad service during a rotation for me. But overall, the last six weeks had provided a kind of get-to-know-you period. A horrible, Purgatory-like period, sure, but in retrospect, it was probably a good thing we'd had the time. We'd even had our first and second fights, one mild and one higher on the scale of intensity. After the fact, we both agreed it'd been good to fight since that was part of a relationship. Also after those, I honestly looked forward to fighting in person, though I didn't imagine it would happen all that often.

In the meantime, she'd resigned at her school, deferred her master's program for a year, and sold off most of her furniture. She'd even interviewed for three different jobs on post, and as chances would have it, got the one I'd seen advertised at the Ed Center. Since I wasn't PCSing, we had to pay out of pocket for any of her stuff she wanted to move. Since she'd sold almost everything but her clothes and a few trinkets and hadn't started our marriage with much after fleeing from her family, a few suitcases and some boxes shipped to the APO had done the job.

I'd worked with the housing office to find a small apartment in town. They'd found us a nice one. And though I'd have to get used to waking up more than ten minutes before PT in the morning, I figured if I woke up next to Katie, it'd be worth it.

Every item we checked off the to-do list made me more desperate for her to get here and stay. A happy byproduct of all this was that Sergeant Major Allen's suspicions seemed to have been abated by my request for married housing. Apparently, living with your spouse knocked you down a peg on the suspicion radar.

When she walked out of the airport terminal looking like the most beautiful thing I'd ever seen—*ever*—I did what I'd wanted to do for months now. I hugged her tight to my chest, kissed her, and dropped to one knee.

Her gorgeous brown eyes studied me, letting out a giggle as her cheeks turned a shade of pink.

"I love you, Katie Miller. Would you do me the honor of... continuing to be Katie Miller? Will you be mine, and wear this ring as a symbol of the new commitment we've made to each other?" I pulled out a new ring, one with a decent-size diamond this time.

"You're crazy," she said, her hands and voice shaking as she tugged on me to stand.

"About you? Yes."

She chuckled. "Okay. I'll wear your ring, Noah Miller."

"Good answer, Mrs. Miller."

EPILOGUE

Nate Reynolds

Eric rubbed at his temples and looked surprisingly aged.

"You look old when you do that." Why keep it inside when it's just got to get out?

He speared me with a glare. "Not helpful."

I sighed dramatically, my knee bouncing where I sat slumped in the chair in front of his desk. "I know. I just don't want to be dealing with this. Why do people have to be idiots?"

We'd had a run of ridiculousness lately. Drunk driving, a lieutenant who straight up needed substance abuse counseling, and a host of other issues.

He shook his head wordlessly, clicking and scrolling on his mouse, his attention directed at the monitors on his desk. "I don't know. But we've got to at least do a sit-down with some of these guys. I want to make sure we nip this in the bud."

I shuddered. "*Nip this in the bud* is also a very old-mannish thing to say, for the record."

"For your mother's record," he grumped.

I chuckled. "I'll do it."

"Good. We also need to get Wild in here to—"

A knock came at the door and Noah Miller stepped through. "Sorry to interrupt."

"Ah, good. Come on in. I have your leave form right here. Meant to bring it out to you," Eric said, waving the man over to his desk.

"Thanks, sir."

"Where are you heading?" I asked as Miller waited for Eric to find the right paperwork.

"It's, uh, a honeymoon of sorts. We never got one when we got married. So we're doin' a Mediterranean cruise." His cheeks reddened and he shifted from foot to foot.

"Ah, that'll be great. Congratulations." Good for him. Truly. He deserved some peace and happiness.

"Thanks. And thank you, sir, for givin' me leave. I know I've taken a lot lately, and I appreciate this more than I can say."

Eric straightened behind his desk and presented the papers to Miller. "You've got enough leave to take a month and then some if you wanted. I'm glad this one falls between rotations, so it's an easy yes. Have a great time."

Miller nodded. "Roger, sir. Will do. Please pass along my thanks to your wife for all the help she's been."

Eric nodded, and Miller turned for the exit, but I couldn't resist a chance to ask.

"Miller, can I ask you a question?" I stood, glancing at Eric to see him nod. He knew what I wanted.

"Of course."

"Any chance you know what's going on with Captain Wild? I know he's a friend..." I trailed off, hoping he'd fill in the blanks.

"Oh." He cleared his throat. "Normally, I wouldn't say anything, but doin' a heap of work in therapy makes me resist the idea I shouldn't speak up if I'm worried, especially now that you've asked. I don't know exactly what's up, but I think he's in a rough patch."

Eric and I both nodded, recognizing this as truth from what we'd observed.

"Thanks. Have a great trip."

Miller left, and I sat back down, but Eric stayed standing and scrubbed at his eyes. "Damn."

"Yeah. It's fine. I'll check in on him, and we've likely got good news for him soon, anyway."

"True."

"That's enough now. You need to head home and pack, and go take your wife on her honeymoon."

His face beamed, that same huge smile he got whenever he thought of his new wife. He and Livie had married on Malta a month ago. They'd decided they just didn't want to wait, so during the summer block leave, we'd all flown out for the destination wedding. I was honored to be the best man, and Livie's friends, including Ariel, were bridesmaids. Her parents made the trip and were genuinely delightful. Delia and Robby were the flower girl and ring bearer, but they both got to stand up with Livie and Eric, and it was, admittedly, a very sweet ceremony.

In fact, it had nearly brought me to tears. Not that I prided myself on not crying or anything stupid like that. Real men cry, just like women. But I didn't expect to get choked up. The night before at the rehearsal, my throat had tightened when Livie had walked down the aisle. I should've known then.

Seeing Eric so happy after the years recovering from his divorce, and honestly, a totally dead marriage since I'd met him eight years prior, felt like someone had turned on the sun. It'd been a celebration of the triumph of love, and my heart genuinely burst with joy for the whole family.

If the bursting heart hadn't been enough, in the quiet of the evening after the wedding, I'd walked on the beach, wrestling with darker thoughts. I'd tried to resist the turn inward, but nothing could keep the inevitable away. The questions for myself. When would I have that?

When, if ever, would that be me?

I exhaled, shaking off the memory when he spoke.

"All right then, my friend, you're it. Keep me posted on anything I need to know, but otherwise, you're officially CO until I'm back." He winked at me, then shuffled together a few papers and tucked them into his planner.

I slipped out of the chair I so often occupied across from his and paused at the doorway. "Have fun. I'll let you know what happens with Captain Wild."

I hope you loved sweet Noah and Katie! Keep reading for a sneak peek of the next Soldiers Overseas Romance Series book starring Bec Jones and Thatcher Wild, Fight After Flight, and get your copy today!

ALSO BY CLAIRE CAIN

Veterans of Silver Ridge Series

Small Town Veteran Romance

Love Undercover

Romantic Suspense Light

Back to Silver Ridge Series

Small Town Romance

Exceptional Mission Unit: The Cardinals

Military Romantic Suspense

The Silver Ridge Resort Series

Small Town Romance

Soldiers Overseas Romances

Sweet Military Romance

The Rambler Battalion Series

Sweet Military Romance

Married to the Military Series

Military Marriage of Convenience Romcoms

ACKNOWLEDGMENTS

First, thanks to the readers who've chosen to spend time with Noah and Katie!

Thank you to my kids, husband, and parents, all of whom support me so unconditionally, while still telling me the truth.

Thank you to my beta readers Emma and Caroline. This book is better because of your feedback. Also I love reading your beta sheets because they are hilarious. Thank you for giving your time to this book!

Thank you, Jamie, as always, for being the tops. Thanks especially for telling me to keep going, to learn and grow and not sit down in the sad, even when it was hard!

Thanks to Zee Monodee for editing this book and pushing for more between Noah and Katie.

Thanks to Amanda Cuff for improving the clarity and focus of the work from the sentence-level on up.

Thank you to Rainbeau Decker for finding gorgeous people and photos for every book!

Thank you to Emma for your thoughtful design, your endless support, and your friendship. WOW.

Thanks to Julie for being the adult in the room for me during the writing of this book, and for walking through the challenges that came with it in life and art.

Thanks to Claire's Sweet Readers for cheering this book on, and keeping me going!

ABOUT THE AUTHOR

Claire Cain lives to eat and drink her way around the globe with her traveling soldier and three kids, but is perhaps even happier hunkered down at home in a pair of sweatpants and slippers using any free moment she has to read and cook. Or talk—she really likes to talk. She has become an expert at packing too many dishes in too few cabinets and making houses into homes from Utah to Germany and many places in between. She's a proud Army wife and is frankly just really happy to be here.

You can also join Claire's facebook reader group for exclusive content and fun: https://www.facebook.com/groups/clairecain/

Website: http://www.clairecainwriter.com

E-mail: Claire@ClaireCainWriter.com

Newsletter sign-up for new releases, exclusives, and freebies: http://www.clairecainwriter.com/newsletter

SNEAK PEEK - FIGHT AFTER FLIGHT

Bec

Muffled voices hummed outside my office door. Each echo set the cadence to which my heart pounded, shooting adrenaline through me in rough, angry jolts that caused my hands to shake.

The handle on the door lowered. My breath evaporated, if that was a thing breath could do. Like it got robbed from my lungs. I couldn't catch it—it ran away like a coward. Not unlike me.

And there he was.

"Bec."

I blinked, the sound of his voice harsh and beautiful. Familiar and yet new. I stood.

"Thatcher."

His face—one I'd known to be typically smiling and kind and warm and wonderful, right up until the last few weeks before I'd left—looked older. His eyes, like his skin, were still deep brown, the gaze probing, the cut of his cheeks and jaw masculine and appealing, his lips sculpted and, I knew, ever so soft. He still shaved his head like he had before, the dark curve of his skull serving to highlight his beautiful face all the more.

But today, notably, no welcoming crinkle feathered at the side of his eyes, nor did those lips curve up into a smile. I couldn't see his perfect white teeth. I couldn't see much of the man I'd known.

His dark brows dipped low. "What are you doing here?"

I blinked again, insides frozen. "I work here."

He shook his head slightly, like he didn't mean to say what he had. "I mean, what are you doing working *here* at Kugelfels? I thought you were in Belgium or something."

He'd thought of me? Had ideas about where I should be? Somehow, this only made me feel more wretched, especially after the way I had treated him. "I considered it, but then this position opened and I wanted to come here because Emily Wender, the director, was my old boss at Fort Campbell."

The words *Fort Campbell* fell hard into the room. The air seemed to flatten out under their weight, and my breath, which had returned out of thin air, came out in a pant. My hands shook and I folded my arms across my chest, tucking them in tight for protection.

"It's…" he trailed off, then licked his lips. "It's good to see you, Bec."

I wanted to close my eyes against his words. Why was this was hitting me so hard? But oh, God, it was.

"I—you too."

What else could I say? *I've dreamed about this?* Or, *I've dreaded and longed for this in equal measure?* Or better yet, *I missed you so much it hurt?*

I couldn't. I wouldn't.

The tightness in his posture relaxed a bit, his shoulders and neck less rigid now. "This is crazy. After all this time..."

His eyes roamed over my face, and some of that light, sweet quality he'd always had entered his expression. My stomach flipped, his eyes on me no less affecting than they'd ever been.

"Yeah," I scraped out.

He smiled. Just a closed-mouth smile, but it slapped at me, reminding me of too many things.

Memories of meeting him before he and Ben and my twin brother Dillon deployed. Memories of seeing him after —after Dillon had died and I became a venerated Gold Star Family member. The crashing, aching loss fisting my heart in a vise so unforgiving, I hadn't felt it so strongly in years.

"Well, listen, I know it's closing time. I just—I saw you and had to say hi. Let's grab coffee and catch up sometime."

Meet with him. Again? That superhuman strength I did not possess. I crushed my teeth together, my jaw aching with the contact. When I spoke, it was breath and air more than sound, the effort to speak one I hadn't realized would be such a challenge. "I, uh..."

He tilted his head, his smile patient. "Why don't we exchange numbers and we can arrange it that way. I'm sure you've got to—"

"No."

The sound of my voice cut through the room, and my eyes widened at how cold it sounded. But I needed him to leave, and I didn't want his number. I didn't want coffee with him. And how could he possibly want it with me?

His expressive face didn't hide his response. His brows rose, and surprise, a flash of hurt, then frustration settled there.

"Okay..." he said, sounding confused.

"Sorry. I just... I can't."

His mouth opened, then shut, and his lips flattened into a grim line. "Okay then."

He left, and the door swung shut. I collapsed into my chair, spent from what had been mere minutes. But these had been minutes with Thatcher Wild, which gave the time a whole other draining, intense dimension I was not ready for.

Fight After Flight is available now!